# FATAL

# CHOICE

## Books by Dorothy Howell

## The Haley Randolph Mystery Series

HANDBAGS AND HOMICIDE

PURSES AND POISON

SHOULDER BAGS AND SHOOTINGS

CLUTCHES AND CURSES

SLAY BELLS AND SATCHELS

TOTE BAGS AND TOE TAGS

EVENING BAGS AND EXECUTIONS

DUFFEL BAGS AND DROWNINGS

BEACH BAGS AND BURGLARIES

FANNY PACKS AND FOUL PLAY

SWAG BAGS AND SWINDLERS

## The Dana Mackenzie Mystery Series

FATAL DEBT

FATAL LUCK

FATAL CHOICE

# FATAL

# CHOICE

# DOROTHY HOWELL

ISBN: 10-0-985-6-9306-1
Published in the United States of America
Fatal Choice

*With love to Stacy, Judy, Seth, and Brian*

## Acknowledgments

The author is extremely grateful for the love, support, and encouragement of many people. Some of them are: Stacy Howell, Judith Branstetter, Seth Branstetter, and Brian Branstetter.

A special thanks for their expertise goes to Evie Cook, Richard Hayden, Webcrafters Designs, and William F. Wu, Ph.D.

# Chapter 1

When your phone rings at three in the morning, something's wrong.

At that hour, it's too late for your friends to call insisting you join their party or for an ex-boyfriend to drunk-dial you, and it's too early for a family member with bad news to wake you or for a telemarketer who doesn't understand time zones to try to sell you solar panels.

So when my cell phone rang a little after three on Monday morning—which still seemed like Sunday night to me—I didn't even look at the caller ID screen. I just answered.

"Hello," I said.

At least, I meant to say it. Even though I knew something must be wrong if I was getting a call at this hour, I was snuggled under the covers, warm in my bed, so the part of my brain that understood the situation hadn't yet alerted the rest of my senses.

"Dana!"

I recognized my friend Jillian's voice. She sounded outraged, angry, and panicked—but mostly outraged and angry. We'd been friends for many of my 27 years on this planet so I knew there was no reason to ask what was wrong. She'd tell me.

"You're not going to believe what that jerk did!" she screamed.

I pushed myself up on my elbow and swept my hair off my face.

"He left me!" she yelled. "*Left* me! Just *left* me!"

Seven Eleven, my sweet little tabby and the only living thing I'd shared my bed with lately, roused and stretched.

"What a jerk! I can't believe this!" Jillian shouted.

I sat up and Seven Eleven slunk over and curled up in my lap. I rubbed my eyes and yawned.

"Can you believe it?" Jillian demanded.

I was partially asleep but still lucid enough to recall that Jillian wasn't involved in a relationship with a jerk, or anyone else for that matter, who would have just *left* her.

"You're ahead of me," I said. "What's going on?"

Jillian huffed, annoyed now with me as well as whoever the jerk was and the situation she'd found herself in. I wasn't offended.

"Brett," Jillian told me. "You know, Brett. That totally hot guy we've been talking to for the last few weeks."

A number of my brain cells awoke and presented me with the image of the tall, blonde, early-thirties, well dressed, handsome guy Jillian and I had chatted with—and she'd flirted with—at a wine bar we frequented. Brett Something.

My brain cells forged head and presented me with another, much less desirable image.

"He was there last night?" I asked.

We'd been at the wine bar with some friends and I'd gone home ahead of everyone else because I had to go to work the next morning—which was now *this* morning.

"You went home with him," I realized. "Back to his place?"

"Yes! And what a jerk he turned out to be!" Jillian yelled. "I woke up a few minutes ago and he's not here. He's gone!"

"Maybe he's in the bathroom," I said.

"No," she insisted. "His clothes are gone. His cell phone is gone. His keys are gone. I looked out the window and his car isn't in the driveway. It's gone, too."

"Did he leave you a note? Text you?" I asked. "Anything?"

"Nothing," she told me. "He left. That's it."

"He sneaked out of his own house and left you there alone?" I said. "Yeah, that's a jerk thing to do."

"I've got to get out of here," Jillian told me.

She sounded less angry and outraged now, more panicky.

"I don't want to be here when he decides to show up," she said. "I might seriously kill him if I see him again."

"Understandable," I agreed.

"I left my car at the bar," Jillian said. "You *have* to come and get me. Please, Dana, you have to."

I eased Seven Eleven off of my lap and said, "What's the address?"

"I don't know," Jillian wailed.

"You don't know where you are?" I asked.

"He drove! I wasn't paying attention—why would I? I never thought he'd run off and leave me stranded!"

"Okay, calm down," I said, pushing off the covers and climbing out of bed. "Where are you, exactly?"

"Upstairs in the bedroom," Jillian said.

"Look around. There must be a place where he keeps his mail. Find a utility bill or a credit card statement or something. It'll have the address on it," I said.

While Jillian searched the house I wedged my cell phone between my ear and shoulder and changed out of my pajamas into jeans, a sweater, and boots.

Jillian came back on the line. "I found it," she said.

She read the address to me and I tapped it into my cell phone. "I'll be there soon," I told her and ended the call.

I grabbed a hoodie from my hall closet and pulled it on, picked up my handbag and car keys off of my kitchen table, and left.

It was three in the morning, cold outside, I didn't know the neighborhood I was heading to, and I had to be at work in a few hours.

Jillian was my friend. What else could I do?

\*\*\*

Even here in sunny Southern California, January nights were chilly. I pulled my hood over my head as I left my apartment on the second floor, skipped down the stairs, and followed the walkway to the parking lot. The air was still and crisp. No one else was out. Two windows were lighted in the building next to mine.

I punched Brett's address into Google Maps as I climbed into my Honda. The seats were cold. I backed out of the spot, drove through the complex, then turned left onto a side street and stopped at the traffic signal at State Street. Headlights pulled up behind me.

I blew into my hands until the light changed. The car on my rear bumper followed me through the turn. I wondered what had brought the driver out at this hour.

I headed east on State Street. It was one of the main arteries through Santa Flores. Signs and security lighting burned at the businesses on both sides of the street, but at this hour, everything was closed.

Santa Flores was located about half way between Los Angeles and Palm Springs. Like most places, there were upscale areas, scary neighborhoods, and everything in between. Thanks to a long run of economic downturns, Santa Flores was heavy on scary, light on everything in between, and short on upscale.

Still, it was the place I called home and had all my life. My mom and dad, and some other relatives, lived here. Only my older brother had flown the nest after he'd gotten married. He lived up north. Everyone was good with it except Mom who, just because she's Mom, *knew* he planned to move back.

A little tremor of guilt and dread caused me to shiver at the thought.

Businesses along State Street became sparse as I continued east. So far I'd passed only a half dozen vehicles. Whoever had been behind me had dropped back.

Since I was fully awake now—thanks in no small part to the inevitable conversation I'd have to have with my mom, the mere thought of which made me queasy—I realized the address Jillian had given me was in Maywood, an area of upscale housing tracts situated to the east of Santa Flores on acreage where orange groves once thrived. I drove several miles more before the GPS instructed me to turn off of State Street, then directed me through several residential streets to Ingalls Avenue.

Brett's neighborhood was nice. Large one- and two-story homes on slightly bigger-than-expected lots, with mature landscaping expertly trimmed and carefully tended. Not as grand as some of the areas in Maywood, but really nice—at least as much of it as I could see by streetlight.

When the GPS announced I was approaching my destination, I half expected to see Brett's car parked in his driveway. Obviously, something had caused him to get out of bed with Jillian and leave her there alone, and he might have returned by now.

With that thought came the flash that he'd come back, smoothed things over, Jillian had forgiven him, and I'd made this trip for nothing. If so, I wouldn't be mad at Jillian. Friends didn't get mad at each other for something like that. Annoyed, yes, but not mad. Besides, I didn't have much longer to come to her rescue on a moment's notice.

I pulled up to the curb in front of the house and killed the engine. Mine was the only car there, so I figured Brett hadn't returned, unless he'd parked inside the garage.

I got out of my Honda. No lights burned in the windows at Brett's house. The surrounding homes were dark. The neighborhood was silent. Not even a dog barked when I shut my car door.

As I headed up the walkway to the front door, I hoped Jillian was waiting in the foyer, ready to leave. I had to be at work in a few hours and Mondays were tough, even on a full night's sleep. Hopefully, I could drop her off and go back to bed.

I knocked, waited a minute or two, then rang the bell. The door jerked open. Jillian glared out at me.

I'm tall, blue eyed, and dark haired. Jillian was short, brown eyed, and now my complete polar opposite since she'd recently gone blonde.

"Can you believe this?" she demanded, as I stepped inside. She shut the door. "I can't believe this."

Faint light from somewhere in the rear of the house cast the entryway in a gray gloom, throwing shadows across a curio cabinet, a grandfather clock, and the tile floor.

"What a total jerk," Jillian railed, and flung out both arms.

She had on the same short black skirt, red sweater, and three-inch pumps I'd seen her in last night when I'd left the wine bar. Her makeup was streaked and mascara smudges darkened her eyes. We both had a serious case of bedhead going, but thankfully mine was covered with my hood.

"Why would he do this?" she said. "Why would he get up and walk out?"

It occurred to me to suggest that Brett might have bolted to help a panicked friend who'd called in the middle of the night, but I didn't think Jillian would appreciate the irony.

"Who just leaves?" Jillian demanded.

This situation gave every indication that it would be discussed at great length for many days to come. Jillian wasn't going to get over it any time soon.

"Let's get out of here," I said. "Where's your handbag?"

"Oh my God, I don't know," she moaned, looking around the entryway. "When we got here last night I was kind of, you know, sort of …."

"Drunk," I said, which explained why she'd left her car at the wine bar.

Jillian drew herself up. "Seriously, I've got to get out of this house. If he comes back, I'll kill him."

I gestured to the staircase leading to the second floor. "Did you leave it up there?"

"No, no, I made sure I got everything," she said, then squeezed her eyes closed for a few seconds. "Maybe I left it in the kitchen. We had some wine when we got here."

Jillian headed off to the right and I followed her through the dining room, which was lit by a tiny night light. Crystal and china sparkled in a hutch situated next to a long table. She pushed open a swinging door to the kitchen and, a few seconds later, harsh light flooded out.

"Thank God. There it is." Jillian disappeared from view.

"Grab it and let's go," I said, and headed back toward the foyer.

Jillian screamed. I whipped around, bumped into the china hutch, then rushed into the kitchen.

She stood in the center of the room, her eyes wide with terror, fists clenched, screaming.

At her feet was a woman. Blood pooled around her head.

I knew right away she was dead.

# Chapter 2

"Oh my God, is she … is she—dead?" Jillian asked, moving away from the body. "Is she breathing? I don't see her breathing."

The woman lay on her side, her head turned away. She was tall and thin, wearing jeans, sneakers, and a black jacket.

I inched closer, careful not to step in the pool of blood, then pulled my sleeve over my fingers and pressed them against her neck. Nothing.

"She's dead," I said, straightening up and backing away. "Who is she?"

"How would I know?" Jillian demanded.

I eased around the body to get a better look. Her eyes were closed, as if she was sleeping, and her short dark hair was soaked with blood. I guessed her age at late twenties, maybe thirty already. I'd never seen her before.

"Do you think she just fell and hit her head and died?" Jillian asked, as if afraid to hear the answer. "Or was she, you know, murdered?"

I glanced around the kitchen. It was as upscale as would be expected for a home in this neighborhood, fitted out with granite countertops, stainless steel appliances, and pearl white cabinets.

Pots and pans were scattered across the floor along with shards of glass and broken plates. Drops of blood were splattered on the cabinets and the door that lead to the garage. There'd been a struggle here and the woman, whoever she was, had put up a fight until what looked like a blow to the head had ended it.

"This was no accident," I said.

"Where's Brett?" Jillian asked, looking around the kitchen. "Is he here somewhere … dead?"

I shook my head. "His car is gone. You said his wallet, phone, and keys weren't upstairs. He must have driven off."

"And left me here with a dead body in the kitchen?" Jillian screamed.

She was close to losing it. I wasn't feeling so great myself.

"Why would he do that?" she shouted. "Why would he leave? What was he thinking?"

The answer seemed obvious to me.

"Maybe he's the one who killed her," I said. "Why else would he run away?"

"Oh my God, we've got to get out of here."

Jillian bolted for the door to the dining room, but I blocked her path.

"We can't leave," I told her. "We have to call the police."

"No." She shook her head frantically. "No. No! I don't want to get involved in this."

"You're already involved," I said. "People at the wine bar saw you and Brett together. They probably saw you leave with him. Your fingerprints and DNA are in his car, they're all over the house. The detectives will find out you were here. How's it going to look if you run away?"

"This is a nightmare." Jillian covered her eyes with her palms and shook her head. Her eyes popped open. "Oh my God, what if the cops think we're involved? What if they think we did it?"

"Neither of us have any of her blood on us, or scratches or bruises from a fight. There's nothing to implicate us," I said. "We don't even know who she is."

I didn't add that, even without a rush to judgment, it wouldn't be hard for the police to surmise why Brett *wasn't* here.

Jillian was quiet for a moment, thinking. Then she glanced back at the woman lying on the floor.

"It wouldn't be right to just walk out and … leave her like that," she said.

"Where's your phone?" I asked. "I left mine in the car in my purse."

Jillian patted the side pockets of her skirt, and pulled out her cell phone. She drew in a breath and looked down at the keypad. She paused, her thumb poised to punch the buttons, then lowered her phone.

"You should leave," Jillian said.

I wondered if she was more rattled than I'd thought.

"I just explained that we have to stay—"

"I have to stay. You don't," Jillian told me. "There's no reason for you to get involved in this."

—

"Too late for that," I said.

"No. Not really," she said. "Nobody knows you're here, except me. You haven't touched anything. You haven't left any of your fingerprints or DNA, or whatever, anywhere in the house."

"That's not the point," I told her.

"There's nothing you can tell the cops that I can't," Jillian said. "You don't need to be here."

"I'm not going to just walk away and leave you here to handle this by yourself," I said.

Jillian gave me the first sensible look I'd seen from her since I'd gotten here and said, "Have you forgotten about your whatever-you-call-it for that company in Pasadena?"

Actually, I had forgotten. Her reminder hit me hard.

"You can't let that get screwed up, Dana," Jillian said. "Not for something like this."

"But—"

"It's too important," she said.

"No—"

"Come with me," Jillian insisted, and left the kitchen through the swinging door.

I followed her across the dining room to the windows that faced the street. She peered out through the plantation shutters.

"Look," she said, stepping back. "Nobody is outside. There's not one single light burning in any of the neighbors' windows. You haven't been seen here—you've only been in the house, what, not even ten minutes."

I looked out the window and saw that Jillian was right. The neighborhood was as silent as when I'd pulled up.

Still, it didn't seem right to leave although, honestly, I couldn't think of one single thing I could add to the homicide detectives' investigation.

"It's not worth it," Jillian said. "You've got a lot on the line right now, Dana. Don't mess it up because of this."

I hesitated and said, "It would be selfish for me to go."

"You'd do it for me," Jillian pointed out.

She was right. I would.

I'd jumped out of bed at three in the morning to help her. I shouldn't be surprised she was doing the same for me—especially since the stakes were so high.

"You're getting out of here," Jillian declared, and hooked my

9

arm through hers. She walked with me to the entryway and opened the front door. "Go, will you, so I can call the cops and get this over with."

I looked outside. It was dark. No one walked the streets. No cars drove past.

I didn't like leaving a crime scene—especially one that involved my best friend, no matter how remotely. But, really, there was nothing more I could do here. I had no info for the detectives.

I had, however, been dealing with that company in Pasadena for weeks. My involvement with a murder investigation—no matter how innocent—wouldn't look good. It could, in fact, blow the whole thing for me.

"Go," Jillian said.

"You're sure?"

"Positive."

I hesitated a few more seconds, then said, "Call me later."

"I will," she promised.

I hurried to my car, jumped in and sped away.

\*\*\*

January was hard. Mondays were hard. A Monday morning in January when you're tired, guilt ridden, and worried was the worst.

That's how it felt when I pulled into a parking space in the lot at Mid-America Financial Services where I worked in downtown Santa Flores.

After I'd returned to my apartment I'd fallen into bed but I hadn't slept. I couldn't get Jillian and the woman who'd been murdered off my mind.

Who was she? Why had she been there? Why had Brett killed her? It scared me to think that whatever was between her and Brett had turned so violent.

It scared me to think my best friend had spent the night with someone capable of murder.

I still didn't feel good about having left Jillian at the house to face the police alone. It was obvious who the murderer was, making Jillian's involvement in the investigation minimal, and I knew she could handle the situation. Still, it didn't sit right with me to just leave, even though her reasoning had made perfect sense.

As I dragged myself out of my car I glanced at my cell phone. No text message or call from Jillian. I thought she would have contacted me by now.

Surely, the homicide detectives and the lab techs had finished gathering evidence, taken statements, and finished with whatever else had to be done. It had been hours.

Maybe I was worrying for nothing, I decided as I crossed the parking lot. Jillian had probably gone straight home and fallen into bed. She'd call me as soon as she woke up.

I unlocked the office door with my key. Mid-America, the place that consumed my time, energy, and effort forty-plus hours each week, was a nationwide company that made personal and home equity loans, and did dealer financing for high-end appliances and electronics. I went inside and locked the door behind me; employees reported to work a half hour before we opened to the public at nine, so everyone had a key.

Carmen, our cashier, sat behind the front counter. She was a few years younger than me but was already married with a family of her own. Pretty with long dark hair, she managed to make our customers feel welcome while handling her clerical duties with ease.

She gave me a tight smile—not a great way to start a Monday morning.

"We have company," she whispered.

That could only mean one thing—the district manager was here.

This was definitely not what I needed this morning and it didn't bode well for the week ahead. Upper management seldom dropped by to tell us we were doing a great job.

My gaze hopped from desk to desk in the large room where we all sat amid office-bland beige carpet, walls, and furniture, and seascapes in plastic frames. All the branch employees were in place, shuffling papers around instead of chatting about the weekend and waking up with breakroom coffee. The door to Mr. Burrows' private office stood open. He was our branch manager, an old-school guy who always dressed in three-piece suits and kept his gray hair and mustache clipped short. He spent most of his time out of the office, so we almost never saw him—my kind of supervisor.

As I headed toward the rear of the office I spotted Mr. Frazier, the district manager and the last person any of us wanted to see on a Monday morning. He was a good ten years younger than

Mr. Burrows, with a solid build, dark hair, and a zest for finding mistakes and making everyone's life miserable over them. He stood behind Mr. Burrows yammering and pointing to his computer screen.

Our office was on the ground floor of a two-story building and we shared the parking lot with the other businesses. If I hadn't been so mired in my own thoughts about Jillian when I pulled into the lot, I would have noticed Mr. Frazier's car already parked there. Mid-America was part of a mega-conglomerate, so branch managers and above got company cars. This year it was a Buick. Mr. Frazier had selected his in what was probably supposed to be stop-light green but reminded me instead of a big, ugly insect.

"Dana," Inez Marshall said in a low voice as I passed her desk. "Our district manager Mr. Frazier is here today."

A couple of choice words flew into my head but I limited myself to, "No kidding."

"Now, Dana, remember," she said, "it's important we maintain proper office decorum when the DM is here."

Inez was old, really old. She'd worked for Mid-America for decades, never married, never had kids, so the company was her entire life. Her job was to supervise the lending end of the business, which now amounted to only her and one other employee. Inez was also the office manager, one step on the corporate ladder below Mr. Burrows, which meant it was her responsibility to order supplies, monitor time sheets, disseminate corporate memos, and conduct office meetings among other tedious, time-consuming things that nobody else really cared about.

Inez took her duties and responsibilities very seriously—and, for some reason, thought everyone else should, too—and managed to wring what little joy there was out of most everything that happened in the office.

She glanced past me to the wall clock. "You absolutely must be on time when Mr. Frazier is here."

"I'm always on time," I said, which was true—well, mostly true.

"Now, Dana—"

I walked away. It was either that or deliver those choice words.

My little piece of employment heaven was at the rear of the office. Manny Franco, my supervisor, sat at a desk nearby. Manny was slightly overweight, short, and wore his dark hair slicked back in waves. He was always stressed out about something.

"What's Mr. Frazier doing here again?" I asked quietly as I approached.

Manny shook his head. Already his desk was piled up with file folders, and perspiration dotted his brow.

"Something's going down," he murmured.

Mr. Frazier had an office in Riverside, about thirty minutes south of Santa Flores, but he was seldom there. His district comprised ten Mid-America branches spread throughout a number of cities. He traveled from office to office auditing the loans that were granted and verifying that proper collection efforts were being made. He also insured that Mid-America standards were maintained, and state and federal laws were adhered to.

"You think so?" I asked, and glanced into Mr. Burrows' office. Mr. Frazier was still grinding on whatever they were looking at on the computer.

"Got to be," Manny said. "He was here twice in December, then again right after New Year's. Not two weeks later he's back. Something's going down."

"Like what?" I asked.

Possibilities flashed in my head, everything from a change in upper management to someone in our branch getting fired, all of which amped up my anxiety level.

Manny had worked here a lot longer than I had so I hoped he could narrow down the possibilities. Instead he shook his head, my cue to move along.

I settled into my desk and stowed my handbag in my bottom drawer. I didn't want to miss a call or text from Jillian so I kept my cell phone out and set it on vibrate. Inez would likely have a stroke if she saw it, especially with Mr. Frazier in the office, so I slipped it under a file folder on my desk.

The illustrious job title of asset manager had been bestowed upon me when I was hired, which was a fancy way of saying that it was my responsibility to work with customers who'd fallen behind on their payments and help them get their account up-to-date again. I handled collections for the personal loans. Manny was in charge of second mortgages and any of my accounts that blew up into a huge problem.

When I'd taken this job last year I'd been unemployed for a

while. My parents were getting by now, doing well financially. But I remembered some tough times when I was younger so I'd known immediately that Mid-America and I didn't see eye-to-eye on how our customers should be treated.

The faceless corporation that was only interested in their bottom line didn't have to sit across a desk from folks and hear how their lives had fallen apart due to a job loss, medical bills, or an emergency. I did. I understood. So what could I do but put my own spin on the position?

So far, my policy of treating my customers with kindness, dignity, and respect had worked out well. Our month-end figures were always near the top in our district's standings. Of course, there were always a few people who simply refused to make their payments for trumped up reasons of their own. Honestly, there wasn't much I could do, or even wanted to do, to help them.

I logged onto my computer and pulled up my collection route in preparation to start making phone calls and inquiring about late payments. My cell phone vibrated.

I glanced around the office. Neither Manny nor Inez was looking my way. I lifted the file folder and saw I had a text message from Jillian.

Thank God. Finally.

I tapped the screen. The message read, "Outside. Now."

This wasn't what I expected to read. My heart rate shot up.

Grabbing my keys from my purse, I got up from my desk.

"I left something in the car," I said to Manny. I didn't wait for a response.

I ignored Inez's stink-eye as I hurried past, unlocked the door, and went outside. Jillian was in the parking lot pacing behind my Honda, still dressed in last night's outfit.

"You've been with the police all this time?" I asked, as I walked over.

She whirled around. "They think I did it!"

"What?"

Jillian nodded frantically. "The cops. They think I murdered her. They think it was me!"

"Wait, slow down," I said. "What happened? Why would they think that?"

"Because—because she was in Brett's house, and so was I," she said.

"So? What difference does that make?" I asked.
"She's his wife!" Jillian said.
*"What?"*
"The dead girl is Brett's wife!"

# Chapter 3

"Brett is *married?*" I exclaimed. "Did you know?"

"No!" Tears sprang to Jillian's eyes. "Did you? Did he ever mention it? *Ever?*"

I thought back over the past few weeks when we'd been at the wine bar and had seen Brett. He'd seemed at ease there, chatting up the bartenders, table hopping, as if he were a regular. He was doing those things and he had a wife waiting for him at home?

"He never mentioned her," I said. "And he certainly didn't act like he was married, not the way he was always flirting with you."

"I know!"

Jillian pressed her palm against her forehead as tears trickled down her cheeks. She was a mess, I realized, physically and emotionally.

"Have you been at the police station all this time?" I asked.

"Yes! They kept asking me the same questions over and over!" Her eyes widened. "They think I'm involved. They think I murdered her."

"Did they say that?" I asked.

"No, but I could tell by the way they were acting and the things they were saying," she said. "I'm there with Brett. The wife comes home. She's furious. There's a fight, and I kill her. It all makes sense—to them."

"It's one possible scenario," I said. "But it means nothing without evidence."

"They didn't believe a word I said," Jillian told me.

"What about Brett?" I asked.

While I doubted Brett had already blurted out his confession to the homicide detectives, I hoped he'd at least assured them that Jillian had no involvement in the murder.

"He never came back to the house. The cops called his cell phone. No answer. They're looking for him." Jillian gulped.

"He'll do the right thing, won't he? He'll tell the police I wasn't involved when he comes back, right?"

"If he comes back," I said.

"Why wouldn't he—oh my God. "Jillian gasped. "You really think Brett did it? You really think he murdered his wife?"

"It makes sense," I pointed out. "When you were upstairs, did you hear anything? An argument? Sounds of a struggle?"

"I didn't hear anything. I didn't even know Brett had left until I woke up." Jillian covered her eyes with her palms for a few seconds. "Oh my God, this is a nightmare. A nightmare!"

She was close to losing it and, really, I couldn't blame her. Now I felt even worse about leaving her at Brett's house to face the cops alone.

"Look," I said. "If the detectives really thought you were involved they would have arrested you already. They're just fishing now. They haven't even processed all the evidence yet."

Jillian shook her head. "You should have heard them. They're sure it's me, that I'm the one who did it."

I could see that I wasn't going to convince her of anything, not in the shape she was in.

"You need to go home and sleep," I said.

Jillian gulped hard a few times and nodded. "Yeah, I should. I'm totally wiped out."

I looked around the parking lot and spotted her white Camry. The wine bar where she'd left her car last night was a block away, and the police headquarters was only another street over so I figured she must have retrieved her car after leaving the station.

"Are you okay to drive yourself home?" I asked as we walked to her car.

"I think so," Jillian said.

She clicked the locks and opened the door, then spun around, her eyes once more wide with horror.

"Oh my God," she wailed. "What if those detectives find something today, some evidence? What if they come to my apartment?"

Her voice got higher and higher, bordering on hysteria.

"I'll never be able to sleep! I'll just lay there and worry!" Jillian grabbed my arm. "You have to call Nick. Please, Dana. He'll know what's going on, or he can find out. You *have* to call him."

---

It was the very last thing I wanted to do, but she was right. I had to call Nick Travis.

***

When Mr. Frazier finally left for lunch, taking Mr. Burrows with him, the tension in the office shot into the stratosphere as soon as the office door swung shut. Everyone was always anxious when anyone from upper management visited the branch, but it was far worse this time.

I sprang out of my desk chair as Carmen left the front counter.

"What's going on?" she asked, as we met in the center of the office.

"Manny thinks something's going down," I said.

We didn't bother to lower our voices.

I glanced back at Manny. He was out of his desk chair, stretching his neck and rolling his shoulders.

Jade Crosby, the finance rep who worked under Inez, pushed back her chair and crossed her legs. She'd worked for Mid-America longer than I had and, honestly, I didn't really like her. She refused to accept the fact that she was a thirty-something mom. She was divorced so everything she wore was get-a-man short and tight. Her blonde hair was long and straight, and she was forever swinging it from shoulder to shoulder.

"We wouldn't be getting all these visits for no reason," she said, twirling her hair around her fingers.

"Maybe Mr. Frazier is upset because we haven't hired another finance rep yet," Carmen said, nodding to the empty desk near Jade's.

Our branch was authorized to hire an additional employee to handle the lending side of the business. Dennis Bowman had quit right after Christmas and no replacement had been hired yet.

"Maybe they're not going to let us get another finance rep," Jade said. "Maybe that's why Mr. Frazier is here."

"Holy crap," Manny said, joining us and shaking his head. "Corporate could be cutting back staff."

"They only do that if a branch isn't performing well," Jade said.

"Do you think they'll fire Mr. Burrows?" I asked.

"Maybe they'll close our office," Manny said.

Carmen gasped. "Does that mean we'll all get laid off?"

Inez whirled around in her chair and said, "I think this is a good time for us all to review our timesheets."

*"What?"* I blurted out. "Are you even *listening* to what's being said?"

Inez pulled off her reading glasses and let them dangle by the chain around her neck.

"I think an office meeting is order," she declared. "I'll schedule one for Wednesday."

Good grief.

"We're upset *today*," I told her. "Right now."

Inez pursed her lips. "This is a routine visit by Mr. Frazier. I've been through a great many of these situations."

All of us, apparently, were afraid she was about to launch into one of her back-in-the-day stories because everybody scattered. I grabbed my handbag from my desk drawer.

"I'm going to lunch," I told Manny and left.

Outside, I headed for my car, then changed my mind and started walking down Fifth Street. The day was Southern California gorgeous. Taking in the sunshine, stretching my legs seemed like a good idea. A big plus was that I'd worn comfy peek-toe pumps today with my black pants and blazer.

The area surrounding Mid-America was occupied by office and government buildings. The court house and post office were nearby. I walked to the corner and crossed the street. Traffic was heavy. Pedestrians crowded the sidewalk.

I moved along with them and turned onto Sixth Street. This area of town had undergone revitalization not long ago and now resembled a Tuscan village. Quaint shops, boutiques, and restaurants were plentiful. Flowers and shrubs were lit with twinkle lights.

The image of Nick Travis filled my head as I walked. My stomach got mushy and my heart ached at the recollection.

The mushy stomach was because Nick was handsome, tall with dark hair and blue eyes, and had a solid build. I'd known Nick since high school. I'd had a major crush on him back then.

The ache in my heart was because Nick and I reconnected a few months ago and both of us had felt major sparks. Then things had turned ugly—and it was my fault.

Well, not all my fault, I decided as I continued down the sidewalk.

Back in high school Nick, a senior, had dated my best friend Katie Jo Miller when we were sophomores. Nick got her pregnant, made her have an abortion, then dumped her and left town.

That's what I, and most everyone else, believed at the time. So when Nick came into my life again last fall—he's a homicide detective and I'd gotten caught up in a murder investigation—I was still angry with him for what he'd done. I couldn't get past it, even when things started to heat up between us.

When I'd finally confronted Nick, he'd been less than understanding. He'd told me it was none of my business and I should get over it. I couldn't, and I told him so. He still refused to come clean.

Finally, he'd confessed. But along with the truth came Nick's anger. I should have trusted him, he'd told me. I should have thought the best of him, not the worst.

That was two months ago. I hadn't seen or heard from him since.

And yes, I should have trusted him. I should have thought the best.

And yes, if he'd been sensitive to my needs and simply told me what I wanted to know when I'd first brought it up, everything would have turned out differently.

We were in some sort of limbo now. Neither of us had made an effort to contact the other. No calls, texts, or emails. I didn't know how to come back from what had happened and, apparently, he didn't either.

Or maybe he didn't want to.

Both of which were reasons on the list of why I'd agreed to leave Jillian to face the cops alone at Brett's house last night. I was afraid Nick might catch the case and show up. I wouldn't have known how to act if he had.

The other reason I'd left, the one Jillian had used to get me to leave, was far easier to deal with.

Santa Flores had been my home all of my life. My family was here. I had friends I still knew going all the way back to kindergarten. Everything, both major and minor, that had happened to me had occurred within the city limits. I knew every inch of the place inside and out. I had a job I liked, an apartment I loved. It was familiar, comfortable, easy.

Which was why I'd decided to leave.

I slipped into a sandwich shop. The place was loud and crowded. I got in line.

For the past few months I'd felt a bit restless. It was the situation with Nick that had finally pushed me over the edge.

The longer we were apart, the more difficult it had become. I'd fantasized about us running into each other at a restaurant, him showing up at my apartment, seeing him on the street. I'd imagined that moment when we saw each other, and how we'd throw ourselves into each other's arms, apologize, vow to put the past behind us once and for all. I looked for him everywhere I went. I played scenario after scenario in my head—how would he look, act, behave? How would I respond?

But I never saw him. And he, apparently, didn't want to see me.

The whole thing was making me slightly crazy. I finally decided I was hurting myself and something had to give. I applied for a job in Pasadena.

Pasadena was about an hour's drive to the west. That's an hour if there's no traffic, which was pretty much unheard of, so I'd have to move there. I could still visit my parents and friends without too much effort. The best part was that, no matter what trumped up scenes filled my head, I couldn't possibly run into Nick there.

The line inched along. When I finally reached the cashier I ordered a turkey on wheat, chips, and a soda. I paid, and was directed to another line.

I didn't know, of course, how I'd break the news to my parents. We were super close, especially Mom and me. It was unusual if a day went by that we didn't talk or text. She missed my brother terribly since he moved up north and I knew she'd be devastated when I told her that I, her only other child, was moving away.

All of this was predicated on my actually getting the job, of course. I'd been through two interviews already and things looked good. I'd signed the authorization for them to do a background check. The company handled contracts with the government so a security clearance was mandatory.

When I reached the pick-up window, I was presented with my lunch on a red plastic tray. I wormed my way through the crowd, went outside, and found an empty table on the patio. It looked like a flower garden, with lots of greenery and splashes of color. The dining area had been enclosed with Plexiglas to cut down on the breeze and street noise. Most everyone else had a dining partner and was involved in conversation.

I unloaded my tray, carried it to the condiment table and added it to the stack. Just as I turned back, something familiar caught my eye. I rose onto tip-toes and peered over the neatly trimmed hedge at the line of cars on Sixth Street that was stopped at the traffic light.

In one of them sat my brother.

My brother?

I blinked twice and leaned closer trying to get a better look, but the light changed and the car pulled away. I watched until it reached the corner, then turned and disappeared.

What was going on? Was Rob in town, or were my eyes playing tricks on me?

I went back to my table, sat down, and unwrapped my sandwich.

The guy I'd spotted was seated on the passenger side of a car I didn't recognize, and I'd only caught a quick glimpse of the side of his face for a couple of seconds so, really, I couldn't be sure. Anyway, if Rob and Denise were in town I'd have already known because Mom would have organized a family dinner. Plus, they were just here at Christmas so why would they come back again so soon?

I sipped my soda and considered all of this, then decided that yes, I could be mistaken—or at the very least, I wasn't thinking clearly.

Still, my thoughts were sharp enough to know what I had to do.

I pushed my sandwich away, got my cell phone from my handbag, and called Nick.

Dorothy Howell

## Chapter 4

The afternoon passed with Mr. Burrows inside his private office—door closed—and the district manager in there with him. They rarely came out, leaving all of us to speculate on what they were talking about and, more importantly, how it would impact us.

Of course, with no way to predict at which moment the office door might open and one or both of them would walk out, we had to actually keep working. No chatting, desk hopping, personal calls, or lingering in the breakroom.

And I never got a phone call back from Nick. t made for a slow afternoon.

I hadn't really wanted to call Nick. With my sights set on that new job in Pasadena my future was pretty well settled, and it didn't include a sort-of boyfriend that I didn't feel good about contacting and who, obviously, had showed no interest in contacting me these past few months.

But what could I do? Jillian was in trouble and I had to help.

When I'd phoned him at lunch, his voicemail had picked up. I'd left a message asking him to return my call. I didn't say why, since there didn't seem to be a good way to tell him that, after all these months, I was contacting him simply to get information that would benefit my friend. It might have come off as shallow which, I suppose, it was.

Still, the fact that the entire afternoon had passed and Nick hadn't returned my call didn't sit right with me. I was antsy and, really, kind of miffed. For all he knew, I could have been drawing my very last breath, or stranded in a gang-infested neighborhood, or even been ready to apologize, beg forgiveness, and hop into bed with him.

The hours finally ground past and at 5:30 everyone shut down their computers and packed up. I headed for the door.

"Is the DM coming back tomorrow?" I whispered to Manny and nodded toward Mr. Burrows' still-closed office door.

"Your guess is as good as mine," he murmured.

"It's not up to us to question the decisions of upper management," Inez announced from her desk. "We should do our jobs, same as always, no matter who's in our branch. In fact—"

"Maybe you should put that in a memo," I told her.

She paused, as if she were actually considering doing just that, so I shot past her and out the door.

I half expected to see Nick standing near my car in the parking lot when I walked outside. My heart rate picked up and one of my all-time favorite, totally trumped up scenarios—the one where he confesses his love and begs for forgiveness—bloomed in my head. But when I rounded the corner of the building, I saw that nobody was in the parking lot except the employees from the other offices.

No Nick. It seemed he was simply going to ignore my phone call.

But that was good, I told myself as I headed for my car. I'd decided Nick couldn't be part of my life, I was making plans to move on, and even if he'd been waiting with two dozen red roses and had confessed his love for me, it wouldn't have mattered—except that I was still going to have to somehow get info on the murder investigation from him.

Employees got into their cars, backed out of spaces and turned onto Fifth Street, but I didn't follow suit. Going home wasn't the least bit appealing. Jillian hadn't texted me all day so I figured she was still recovering from last night. I'd call and check on her later.

But what could I tell her since Nick hadn't returned my call? She was counting on me to come up with some info, and I didn't want to let her down. Luckily, I knew a good place to start looking, so instead of getting into my car I walked over to Sixth Street.

Quota Vino was the wine bar Jillian and I had frequented lately. There wasn't much of a crowd when I walked in, only about a half dozen people scattered throughout the place. It had a definite Old World vibe to it, with exposed brick, tile, and dark woodwork. A bar ran along the left side of the room backed by a mirror and shelves stocked with glasses and bottles. Booths lined the opposite wall. I slid onto a chair at one of the tall tables that filled the space in between, and fished my cell phone from my purse.

Still nothing from Jillian, I saw as I placed my phone on the table. Nick, either. But I'd gotten a message from Mom. She wanted to know how I was doing since we hadn't spoken yet today. I didn't want to tell her the truth, of course, so I texted her back explaining about the district manager's presence in the office. Mom hadn't worked in about thirty years, but I knew she'd understand. Mom always understood. She was that kind of mom.

It flashed in my head again that I wasn't looking forward to telling her about the Pasadena job.

The waitress passed my table with a tray of drinks and gave me a be-with-you-soon eyebrow bob and a quick smile. Because Jillian and I came here often we'd gotten to know her. Shelly was fortyish, tall, with dark hair, and a few too many applications of tanning spray. She spent a lot of time at the gym and showed off her taut arms with a tank top.

"Hey, Dana," she said a few minutes later when she stopped at my table. "How's it going?"

"Not a great day," I admitted.

"Tell me about it," Shelly said. "Crystal didn't show for her shift."

I glanced behind the bar and saw that Gabe was the only other employee on duty, except for the busser who was clearing a table near the entrance. Gabe never seemed rushed, no matter how busy the place got, and tonight was no exception. I figured that was because, judging by his salt and pepper hair, he'd made it into his fifties, had found his pace, and was sticking to it.

"The usual?" Shelly asked.

"Sure," I said.

She headed for the bar and I checked my phone again. Nothing.

I gave myself a mental shake and put my phone into my handbag. I'd come here to get info about Brett. I needed to focus and not keep checking to see if I'd heard from Jillian. Or Nick. Especially Nick.

Shelly stood at the bar while Gabe waited on a couple who'd just sat down in front of him. I'd seen them in here before. In fact, quite a few of the faces around the room looked familiar and that made me think about Brett.

Jillian and I had seen him here probably a dozen times. He'd come by our table and chatted, mostly with Jillian. We'd often had other friends with us so I hadn't paid much attention to the things he'd said, which made me realize now that I really knew very little about him.

Somewhere in the back of my mind I seemed to remember he owned a restaurant. He certainly hadn't mentioned he was married.

Shelly appeared at my table and placed a glass of wine in front of me.

"So, did you hear about Alexa?" she asked and leaned in a little. The blank look on my face prompted her to add, "Brett's wife. You know, Brett Sinclair? His wife was murdered. Last night. Inside her own home."

I decided to play dumb and see what information Shelly might have.

"Oh my God," I said. "You're kidding."

"That's what I heard," she said.

Two women seated at a booth nearby got up and left. The busser hurried over and started clearing their table.

"And," Shelly went on, leaning closer and lowering her voice, "there's a big police investigation."

"How did you find out?" I asked. "Was Brett here today?"

Shelly shook her head. "He's been with the police all day, I'm sure."

It was a logical assumption, but I wasn't going to tell her how wrong she was.

"One of my regulars was in for lunch," she went on. "He's an EMT. He rolled on the call."

"Wow, she was murdered, huh?" I asked. "Do they know who did it?"

Maybe I wouldn't need Nick.

Shelly shrugged. "No clue."

"How's Brett taking it?" I asked.

The busser tapped Shelly on the shoulder and presented her with the bi-fold the women had left on the table.

"Thanks, Flynn," she said, and tucked it into her apron. Flynn went back to wiping down the table. Shelly shuddered, then turned to me again and whispered, "That guy creeps me out. Anyway, I don't know how Brett is handling it. I'm sure he's a mess. I figured that's why Crystal isn't here today."

I was confused and it must have showed on my face because she went on.

"Crystal and Brett used to date," Shelly said, and nodded. "Seriously date. Almost engaged, even."

I felt a little flush of excitement. This could be a major clue. Maybe I could break the case for the detectives.

"Do you think they're together today?" I asked. "Maybe he turned to her for support?"

"Brett doesn't have much family," Shelly said. She rolled her eyes. "I'm sure Crystal offered herself up. She never got over him."

My opinion of Brett dropped a few more notches. Not only was I convinced he was a murderer, but now it seemed he was a first-rate jackass, too.

"Brett would have gone to Crystal for support, even after he'd been flirting with women right in front of her?" I asked.

"I never said Brett was a nice guy." Shelly glanced at the doorway as a couple walked in, then headed toward them.

I was relieved that Shelly hadn't mentioned witnessing Jillian leave the bar with Brett last night. The less people knew about her involvement, the better.

Of course, someone else could have seen them.

I needed to talk to Crystal. Brett might be at her place or, at the very least, she might know where to find him. I didn't know where Crystal lived or how to contact her, but I could find out easily enough.

As I plotted my next move, the busser turned with his tub of dirty dishes and bumped my table. My glass tipped over, shattered, and wine splashed onto my pants leg. I hopped out of the chair.

"Sorry," he mumbled, then cut around me and disappeared through the arched doorway to the kitchen.

I grabbed my handbag and hurried down the narrow hallway to the ladies room. Wall sconces offered faint light and threw shadows over the paintings of vineyards and vintage labels that hung on the exposed brick.

Inside, I used paper towels to soak up most of the wine, then held my leg up to the hand dryer. The hot air took out most of the wetness, but my pants were stained.

"Great," I mumbled to myself as I left the ladies room.

When I stepped into the hallway, a man blocked my path. I gasped and fell back a step, then realized it was Flynn the busser.

"You shouldn't have walked out and left her," he said.

His voice was low. He was only an inch or two taller than me and probably just barely old enough to drink in a bar. His dark hair was combed forward, hiding his forehead but emphasizing his scowl. He looked slightly menacing in the narrow hallway.

"You're supposed to be her friend," he said.

Flynn glared at me for a few seconds, then spun around and left. I stood there, too stunned to move.

Even though Shelly hadn't seen Jillian leave with Brett last night, obviously Flynn had. He must have figured Jillian would be drawn into the murder investigation and blamed me, though why he'd involved himself with the situation, I didn't know.

I took a couple of deep breaths and went back to my table. It hadn't been cleared. Shards of glass littered the table; wine puddled on the floor. I was anxious to leave but I had to take care of something first.

I spotted Shelly waiting on a couple near the entrance. Flynn was wiping down a table nearby, his back to me. Gabe was busy ringing up a drink order. I ducked down the hallway to the kitchen.

Three cooks were busy chopping fruit and veggies at the prep table. Two of them gave me a casual glance as I walked past them to a little alcove with a tiny breakroom, lockers, and a time clock mounted on the wall. There were only a few cards in the slots. I found Crystal's, pulled out my phone and snapped a picture.

Flynn was behind the bar gathering dirty glasses when I walked back into the restaurant. He kept his head down but I was pretty sure I saw him watching me in the mirror. Shelly was still busy with the couple near the entrance. I pulled a ten from my wallet, passed it to her, and left.

The cool air felt good on my face as I walked along Sixth Street. The sidewalk was crowded but traffic had thinned out.

I'd gone to the wine bar to get some information but I'd ended up with more questions than answers.

Why had Brett frequented a place where his ex-girlfriend worked and flirted with other women in front of her? How much more callous and uncaring could he be?

But, really, what kind of ethics was I expecting from a guy who'd murdered his wife and left her dead on his kitchen floor while he had another woman upstairs in his bed?

None of this spoke well of Crystal, either, since she'd continued to endure his despicable treatment. Did she know Alexa was dead? She hadn't showed up for her shift today. Coincidence? I doubted it. More like Brett had gone to her place and she'd taken him in, believing whatever trumped-up story he'd told her.

I'd seen her at the wine bar last night. Obviously, unlike Flynn, she hadn't seen Brett leave with Jillian. Whatever story Brett had told her must have been very convincing if she had, in fact, taken him in. I hoped she wouldn't get dragged into the murder investigation, too.

I waited at the corner until the light changed, then crossed to Fifth Street.

I thought about Flynn. He'd startled me outside the ladies room—and he was a little creepy, as Shelly had said. But he'd hit a nerve. He was right. I shouldn't have gone home early and left Jillian alone in the wine bar last night. If I hadn't, she probably wouldn't have left with Brett and ended up involved in a murder investigation.

The office buildings on Fifth Street had emptied out some time ago. Without the twinkle lights and brightly lit stores and restaurants on Sixth, the street was dark. No one else was around. I walked faster.

A plan to dig up more information on Alexa Sinclair's murder popped into my head, but I doubted I'd have to follow through with it. Everything would be straightened out as soon as the homicide detectives located Brett. He'd run out of his house carrying only his wallet and cell phone. Without a bundle of cash and a burner phone, his movements would be easily tracked online. Even if he refused to confess to his wife's murder, his fingerprints and DNA at the crime scene would confirm his guilt and clear Jillian.

I'd feel better about the whole thing if I knew exactly what the detectives were doing to find Brett, and I might have that information if Nick had called me back.

As I passed the big window at the front of the Mid-America office, I glanced inside. I expected to see Inez seated at her desk preparing memos to distribute tomorrow, but all the lights were off.

I turned the corner of the building to the parking lot. Nick stood beside my car.

Dorothy Howell

# Chapter 5

My heart nearly flew out of my chest. My knees turned to mush and barely held me upright. Breath left me in a wheeze.

Nick. Tall, handsome Nick stood in front of me, not ten feet away. He had on dark trousers and a sport coat over a white shirt and a blue tie that was pulled down; his collar was open. He looked as sturdy and strong as he had the last time I'd seen him two months ago.

My thoughts scattered, along with my emotions. This was the moment I'd fantasized about and dreamed of. Nick seeing me, running to me, holding me, begging forgiveness, and kissing me as he professed his love for me. And now it had happened. The moment was here.

"What are you doing on a dark street by yourself at this time of night?" he said and walked over.

My heart pounded. I couldn't seem to formulate a response.

"It's not safe," he told me. "You should have better sense."

I didn't seem to have any sense at all, at the moment.

"This parking lot is isolated," Nick said, waving his hand around. "The buildings are empty. You've put yourself in a potentially dangerous situation."

I opened my mouth, but no words came out.

What was happening? He was supposed to run to me, sweep me into his arms, apologize, and promise his undying love. Instead I was getting a lecture on urban safety?

"You think I'm in danger?" I asked. "Why? Were you planning to attack me?"

Nick looked at me for a few seconds and then said, "You called me."

So much for his apology and confession of love.

Maybe it was better this way, I decided.

I drew in a breath and focused my thoughts.

"There was a murder last night in Maywood," I said. "A woman named—"

"Alexa Sinclair," Nick said. "Jillian was in for questioning."

Nick had met Jillian last fall. He knew she was my best friend. It irked me that he'd known all day about her involvement in Alexa's murder and hadn't called me.

"So what's going on with the investigation?" I asked.

Nick shrugged. "Not my case."

"Has Brett been located yet?"

"How did you know he was missing?" Nick asked.

He sounded like a cop now, not a friend or an ex-boyfriend, or whatever he was. I knew I had to be careful about what I said.

If during the course of the investigation the homicide detectives really suspected Jillian had murdered Alexa, they would gain access to Jillian's cell phone records and learn that she'd called me last night. But for now, it seemed the cops didn't know about my involvement and I intended to keep it that way—even where Nick was concerned.

"Jillian stopped by after she left the police station," I said, which was the truth, even if it was an incomplete truth. I certainly wasn't going to mention that I'd been asking questions at the wine bar and learned even more about Brett.

Nick was quiet for a moment, then said, "He hasn't been located. Any idea where he is?"

I had no intention of giving up Crystal, so I said, "Probably hiding out somewhere. That's what murderers do."

"You think Brett murdered his wife?" he asked.

"Why else would he take off?" I said. "He killed her, then panicked and ran. It makes perfect sense, right?"

"We detectives try not to make broad assumptions about a case," Nick pointed out.

"Still, you must have some ideas," I insisted.

"Since it's not my case, all I know is that Brett Sinclair hasn't been reached at home, on his cell phone, or at the restaurant he manages."

"I thought he owned the restaurant."

Nick's expression darkened. "Are you involving yourself with the investigation, Dana?"

"My friend is involved. I'm concerned. Why wouldn't I want to know what's going on?"

Nick leaned closer. "I'm telling you right now, you need to keep clear of this investigation—"

He paused and sniffed.

"Have you been drinking?"

Good grief. He smelled the wine that had spilled onto my pants.

Nick frowned. "Have you?"

"No," I insisted.

"Yes, you have," he told me.

I huffed. "One glass, and not even the whole thing."

Nick looked even more troubled now.

"You were at that wine bar, weren't you?" he said. "What were you doing there?"

Obviously, Nick knew more about the investigation than he'd let on if he was aware that Jillian and Brett had been at Quota Vino last night.

But more troubling was the realization that, even though I'd intended not to tell Nick I'd been at Quota Vino, he'd figured it out. He was a good cop—and it was really annoying at times.

"Were you investigating the murder?" he demanded. "That's exactly what you were doing, weren't you?"

"It's none of your business where I go or what I do." I managed to infuse a healthy dose of outraged indignation into my voice.

Nick leaned down until his face was even with mine. Heat rolled off of him. He smelled great.

"I'm making it my business." His voice was low and steady. "I'm not going through this with you again. Not like *last time*."

*Last time* was when I'd gotten involved in a murder investigation. Shots had been fired, my friend had been wounded. I'd put myself in that dangerous situation because I was too angry with Nick to ask him for help.

*Last time* had driven a wedge between us. Our separation had made me crazy with missing him, longing for him, fantasizing about him—and had, ultimately, forced me to make the decision to leave Santa Flores so I could start over without thinking he'd suddenly appear—and fearing that he never would.

Nick stepped back. "Come on. I'll drive you home."

"I don't need you to drive me home," I insisted.

"You get stopped by a cop smelling like that, you'll have a problem." Nick touched my shoulder, urging me forward. "Let's go."

I pulled away. "I'm not leaving my car here all night," I told him.

"I'll drive your car," he said.

"That's crazy," I told him. "How will you get home?"

Nick eased closer. "I'll spend the night at your place."

I froze. Breath went out of me. My gaze met Nick's and I got lost in his warmth, his strength. He touched his finger to my chin and tilted my face up to his. He leaned closer.

I jerked away and headed for my car. He followed but I got there first. I jumped in and backed out of the space.

I buzzed my window down and shouted, "And don't even *think* about following me."

Nick grinned. He's got a killer grin. For an instant it flashed in my head to throw open the passenger side door for him. Instead, I floored it.

I glanced in the rearview mirror as I pulled onto Fifth Street—I could never resist looking at Nick. He stood in the parking lot, watching me.

* * *

"What did you hear?" I whispered as I approached Manny's desk the following morning.

He glanced up from the file he'd been reading. He looked tense—even more tense than yesterday.

"Does it have something to do with Mr. Burrows being late for work this morning?" I asked.

"Holy crap," he whispered. "It's bad."

I'd seen Manny at the file cabinet located next to Mr. Burrows' office a few minutes ago when the district manager, who was on the phone, had abruptly gotten up from the desk and closed the door. Whatever the DM was talking about, he didn't want it overheard.

"How bad?" I asked in a low voice.

Manny glanced around the room and I did the same. Everyone had their head down, working. Tension in the office was beyond the stratosphere, and it was only a little past nine.

"I know why Mr. Burrows isn't in the office yet," Manny said.

This couldn't be good.

I'd brought a file folder with me to Manny's desk for cover, so I eased closer to him and opened it.

Manny stared at the paperwork inside the folder and whispered, "Mr. Frazier was talking to HR."

I struggled not to gasp aloud and keep my gaze glued to the file folder. Anything to do with Human Resources meant something major was going down.

"Sounded like somebody's getting fired," Manny said.

We abandoned all pretense of reading the file folder and looked at each other.

"Mr. Burrows," I realized. "Mr. Frazier sent him out on a call this morning so he could talk to HR about firing him?"

Manny shrugged. "I didn't hear a name mentioned, but that's what it seems like. Mr. Burrows is close to retirement age. They probably want to force him out, get somebody new in here at a lower salary."

"I like Mr. Burrows," I said. "I don't want him to leave."

What I liked about Mr. Burrows was that he was almost never in the office. A new manager might actually want to supervise us. I didn't need, or want, that level of supervision. Dealing with Inez was annoying enough.

"That's why a finance rep hasn't been hired yet. The new manager will do it," Manny said, and jerked his chin toward the front of the office.

I glanced at the desk that had been sitting empty for several weeks, but a flash of blonde caught my eye. Jade's hair was flying from shoulder to shoulder, her a-hot-looking-man-just-walked-in signature move.

Nick flew into my head, ramping up my heartbeat. Had Nick come into the office? To see me? To apologize?

He hadn't followed me home last night, but he might as well have been there. I hadn't been able to stop thinking about him, caught somewhere between insulted and excited about his brazen offer to drive me home and spend the night—especially when the only thing I'd actually curled up with lately was Seven Eleven.

My gaze darted to the front counter and the man who'd come into the office and set Jade's hair in motion. It wasn't Nick. Still, my heartbeat didn't slow down; no woman's would when Slade walked in.

He was ex-Air Force Special Ops, well over six feet tall,

muscular, with blond hair cut short. Today he had on gray cargo pants and a black T-shirt that showed off his washboard abs. Slade worked for Quality Recovery, the company that repossessed cars for us. It was a part-time gig for him. Rumor had it mercenary work in Mexico and the Middle East was also on his résumé.

Jade was rising from her chair, but I was already on my feet. I grabbed the file folder off of Manny's desk, tossed it onto mine, and pushed past her.

"Hi, Slade," I said.

"Hey."

"How's everything going?" I asked, coming around the front counter to stand next to him.

"Cool."

What Slade lacked in verbal skills he more than made up for in looks.

He jerked his chin toward the door. "Got a car for you."

"Well, hello, Slade," Jade cooed as she headed our way, her hair swinging from shoulder to shoulder.

I wasn't about to let Jade get any face-time with Slade. He and I had been through a lot together—strictly professional, of course. But still, there was no way I would allow her to infringe on my time with him.

I might not have Nick, but Slade was mine—even if he wasn't mine-mine.

"Let's check it out," I said to Slade.

I rushed to the door. He followed me outside.

Waiting in our parking lot was a tow truck with Quality Recovery painted on the side and a Chevy Impala dangling from its hook. This wasn't a repossession that involved one of my customers—I seldom had to resort to such measures—but I was still handling it.

The Mid-America branch in Sacramento had contacted me last week about a customer who could no longer make his payments, had moved to our area, and had wanted to surrender the vehicle. The branch manager had asked for help in recovering the Chevy, so I'd called Quality Recovery. Slade had worked fast on this one.

"Looks like it's in good shape," I said, as we walked around the car.

"The owner said it doesn't run. Claimed he couldn't afford to get it fixed," Slade said. "You want an estimate on repairs?"

"Probably," I said. "Let me check with our Sacramento branch. It's up to them. I'll let you know."

I pulled my cell phone from the pocket of my blazer, located the VIN at the bottom of the windshield, and tapped it into the notepad. I snapped some photos of the vehicle. Mid-America needed a record of the condition of the car when it came into our possession, in case there were any questions later on. I'd fill out the company-approved form when I got back inside and send it to the Sacramento branch along with the pics.

"You cool?" Slade asked.

I held up my cell phone. "I have everything I need."

"No," he said. "You. Are you cool?"

You'd be hard pressed to find a more masculine man than Slade—tough, rugged, strong, just the sort of guy who'd kick somebody's butt for you or have your back in a fight. Yet there was a soft streak in him, and I'd been fortunate to be the beneficiary of it on several occasions.

I didn't realize I was giving off a troubled vibe but Slade had seen it. I couldn't lie to him.

"My friend Jillian?" I said.

He nodded.

"She was questioned in a murder that happened in Maywood on Sunday night."

Slade nodded. "Brett Sinclair. His wife."

I wasn't sure where Slade had learned about the murder. I doubted it was from the staff at Quota Vino—Slade wasn't a wine bar kind of guy.

"Jillian discovered the body," I said, and filled him in on what had happened—most of it, anyway.

I didn't feel so good about leaving out my involvement, not where Slade was concerned. But I thought it best. And, if you're going to lie, always tell the same lie.

"The detectives are taking a hard look at Jillian," I said. "I hope they'll locate Brett soon so he can clear her."

"Won't be easy." Slade shook his head. "Sinclair is bad news."

"He killed his wife," I said. "It doesn't get much worse than that."

"Yes, it does."

Slade's tone sent a chill down my spine. His past, at least the rumors of it, flashed in my head and I realized that he'd probably witnessed much worse.

"Stay clear of this one," Slade said.

Nick had given me the same warning last night. Coming from Slade, it didn't annoy me, just made me think he knew something that I—and maybe the homicide detectives—didn't know.

A car pulled into the parking lot. I recognized it immediately, Mr. Burrows in his plain vanilla company car. He rolled into a spot alongside Mr. Frazier's bright green Buick.

Slade must have recognized it, too.

"Later," he said, and climbed into the tow truck.

I headed for the office door. It would have been polite to wait a minute or so for Mr. Burrows to get out of his car but I didn't want to get stuck trying to make small talk with him, not with Manny's suspicion that he might get the ax today still taking up space in my head.

As I approached the office door, my cell phone vibrated in my hand. I looked down at the ID screen. Jillian was calling.

I'd spoken with her briefly last night, just long enough to learn that she'd slept all day, felt awful, and was going back to bed. I hadn't expected to hear from her today. I'd told her Mr. Frazier was in our branch again. She knew what it meant when the entire office was under upper management surveillance—not to mention Inez's watchful eye. Jillian wouldn't call unless it was really important.

I hoped that didn't mean she'd been arrested.

## Chapter 6

"Hang on," I said to Jillian.

I palmed my cell phone when I entered the office. Jade gave me stink-eye as I hurried past her desk and I gave it right back to her, which wasn't very mature of me but I couldn't help myself. Inez gave me stink-eye, too, but I ignored her.

I continued to the breakroom at the rear of the office, then ducked into the restroom and locked the door.

"Jillian, are you okay?" I said into the phone. "You haven't been arrested, have you?"

"Not yet."

She sounded tired and anxious. I couldn't blame her.

"Have the detectives contacted you again?" I asked.

"I haven't heard anything from them. That's probably because they're keeping busy hunting up more things to twist around to make me look guilty," Jillian said. "What about Nick? Did he hear anything? Does he know what's going on with the investigation?"

"He's not on the case, but he knew about it," I told her. "Brett hadn't been located, as of last night."

"The cops haven't found him yet?" she asked, her voice rising. "How can they not find him? Are they really looking for him? Did Nick know? Did he say what they're doing?"

"I'm sure they're doing everything they can," I told her.

I felt really bad that I hadn't come up with more information about the official investigation, so I pushed on.

"Did you know Brett used to date Crystal from Quota Vino?" I asked. "They were serious. Almost engaged."

Jillian was quiet for a few seconds, then said, "He never mentioned it. But the jerk never mentioned his wife, either."

"I'm going to talk to Crystal," I told her. "Brett might have gone to her place last night."

"Really? Do you think he's there? With her?" she asked, sounding a little hopeful.

"He's got to be somewhere," I said. "Have you thought about that night? Have you remembered anything more? Anything at all? Something that maybe seemed a little odd or slightly off?"

"All I've done is relive that whole thing over and over in my head," Jillian said. "Nothing seemed the least bit weird."

"Okay," I said. "Hang in there. I'll call you tonight."

"Thanks, Dana."

We ended the call and I went back to my desk. Mr. Burrows' office door was closed. I figured he was in there with Mr. Frazier, maybe being told he had to retire *or else*.

I was hardly in the mood to work but since I didn't want to find myself in a situation similar to Mr. Burrows' *or else*, I pulled up my phone route and started calling customers. But I couldn't concentrate on their problems, not when I had a huge problem of my own to deal with.

Why had Brett taken Jillian to his home? Sure, it was for the oldest reason in the world, but he could have taken her anywhere—a motel, a friend's place, Jillian's apartment.

Was Brett just plain old cheating on his wife? Was Alexa out of town so he decided to have a little fun—with the added risk of having it in their bed—or were they separated and getting divorced?

Surely, they were. Not even Brett could be that callous—or maybe he could, I thought, given how he flirted with women in Quota Vino right in front of his ex-girlfriend Crystal.

I definitely had to talk to her.

I decided I should talk to Slade again, too. He always knew what was going down in Santa Flores. He didn't seem to think much of Brett. I should find out why, since I didn't have much else to go on.

Glancing around the office, I saw that Inez and everyone else faced their computer screens—one of the benefits of having my desk at the back of the room—and they were projecting the illusion of working diligently so I was free to handle my personal business on the sly.

Maybe having Mr. Frazier in the office had a few benefits.

I opened a file folder on my desk and slid my cell phone beneath it, then tapped the screen until I came to the photo I'd taken of Crystal's timecard in Quota Vino. It showed her full name and the times she'd punched in and out for her shift.

My job of asset manager gave me access to all sorts of data

bases that allowed me to find my customers who'd skipped, or simply moved and hadn't notified us of their change of address. I wasn't supposed to use any of these tools for my personal benefit, of course, but my friend was involved in a murder investigation and to me, that made it worth the risk.

Then I realized I might not have to violate Mid-America's company policy to track down Crystal and talk to her. As I studied her timecard I saw that she worked the same hours most every day. She reported for her shift at three o'clock, and stayed until closing.

She hadn't been at work yesterday. I doubted she could afford to miss another day, even if she was holed up with her ex-lover. A girl's got to eat.

I wanted to catch Crystal outside of Quota Vino as she was reporting for her shift. There would be too many distractions if I tried to talk to her while she was working. That meant timing was crucial—as was coming up with a good reason to leave the office.

I paged through my list of delinquent customers looking for one I could claim had become a problem and required a personal visit from me so Manny would let me leave the office. Before I got halfway through, Inez rose from her desk.

"Attention! Attention in the branch!" she called.

Five of us in the office—including her—and she shouted out an announcement.

Good grief.

"An office meeting will commence immediately!" Inez said.

Manny groaned. "Holy crap."

"All branch employees are to assemble here at my desk at this time," she went on.

"Do we have to?" I grumbled.

I didn't have the time, or the patience, to deal with Inez and one of her office meetings today. I had to make some forward progress on Alexa Sinclair's murder and, eventually, get some actual work done.

Manny just shook his head. I could see there was no way of getting out of Inez's meeting.

Everyone dragged their chair to Inez's desk, exchanging frowns and eye-rolls as we sat down. Inez spent a few minutes getting comfortable, putting on her glasses, then stacking, sorting, and paper clipping several sheets of paper together. She presented them to Carmen.

"Distribute these, please," she said.

Carmen dutifully passed them out, even though we were elbow-to-elbow around Inez's desk.

"I'll start by reading the agenda," Inez proclaimed.

"There's an agenda?" I looked down and saw two items listed. "Come on, Inez, you could have just stopped by our desks and told us this stuff."

She ignored me, adjusted her glasses and said, "Our first item is timesheets. It's extremely important that each employee completes his or her timesheet accurately. Timesheets must be notated immediately upon reporting to the office, and leaving the office."

"We know this already," I said.

"Some employees are not following established procedure," Inez said.

"I always fill out my timesheet," Carmen said.

"It's not like Mid-America will go broke if we're off by a couple of minutes," Jade complained as she combed her fingers through her hair.

"Let's review the proper way to complete a timesheet. I've prepared an example," Inez said. "Everyone please turn the page to the attachment."

"There's an attachment?" I asked, flipping through the pages.

This meeting was never going to end.

I threw Manny a look, as did Carmen and Jade.

"Listen up," Manny said. "Everybody go over the attachment this afternoon. If you have questions, Inez will address them then. Okay, Inez?"

She pursed her lips, clearly disappointed that she couldn't go over the proper completion of the Mid-America timesheet step by step.

Afraid she'd disagree, I said, "You know, Inez, addressing questions one-on-one would make for better training."

I couldn't have cared less about better training, but I had to do something to get the meeting moving.

She pressed her lips tighter and drew her brows together, then finally nodded. "Yes, perhaps you're right. Now, the next item on the agenda is our visit from our district manager Mr. Frazier."

Tension spun up. Carmen's eyes widened, and Jade's fingers stilled in her hair. Manny and I exchanged a worried glance.

---

44

"Mr. Frazier, in his capacity as our district manager, is making a routine visit," Inez explained. "It's not our place to read anything into it, or gossip about it, or start rumors. We're here to do our jobs. That's what we're being paid to do. That's what we should be doing."

We all stared at her.

"There will, of course, be a meeting when Mr. Frazier closes out his branch visit. Everything he comments on will be covered then in detail," Inez went on. "In the meantime, we should all keep working, and strive to do our very best for this wonderful company. The betterment of Mid-America should always be uppermost in our minds and hearts."

Everybody continued to stare—but for a different reason now.

I broke first.

"Are you serious—"

Manny grabbed my elbow.

"No time for Q&A, Dana," he said. "That's it. Meeting's over."

He hoisted himself out of his chair and gave my arm a tug. Carmen and Jade were already scrambling away with their chairs. I got to my feet.

"She is so infuriating," I whispered to Manny as we dragged our chairs to the back of the office.

I was annoyed beyond belief, then realized this might work to my advantage.

"I've got to get out of here," I said. "There's an account in Webster I need to field call. Okay?"

"Sure, Dana, no problem," Manny said.

"I'll go through my route first," I said, as if I were making some great concession for the company's benefit. "I'll go out this afternoon."

"Good. That's good," he said.

I centered my chair behind my desk and sat down, and out of habit checked my cell phone still hidden under the file folder.

Nick had called.

He'd called and I'd missed it because I'd been stuck in Inez's stupid meeting. Now I was doubly annoyed.

Then something else hit me and my thoughts scattered.

Was he calling because he couldn't possibly get through the

rest of the day without hearing my voice? Or was it because he'd learned something new—and troubling—about the Alexa Sinclair murder investigation?

I grabbed my phone and hurried to the restroom. I'd rather have spoken with him in person but I didn't want to wait in case he was giving me a heads-up on something important.

Nick answered on the first ring.

"Did you get home safely last night?" he asked.

His voice was soft and mellow.

I melted a little, okay, more than a little, which was a good reason to keep this professional.

"You called me," I said.

"The investigation is heating up," Nick said, switching to his cop voice. "Things aren't looking good for Jillian."

It felt like a lead weight had crashed down on me.

"What about Brett?" I asked. "Has he been located? He can tell them Jillian had nothing to do with Alexa's death."

"The detectives are focusing on Jillian," Nick said

The lead weight I felt on my shoulders got heavier.

With all the attention on Jillian, the detectives would find their way to her cell phone records, then to the call she'd made to me in the wee hours of Monday morning. They would try to make a connection. Jillian and I could continue to lie about my presence at Brett's house, but would the investigators find some evidence of my being there?

The events of that night whipped through my head and I started to feel queasy as I mentally retraced my steps. When I'd left my apartment, lights were on in two windows of a nearby building. Would the detectives canvas my complex and find someone who saw me leave?

"Dana?" Nick asked.

And what about my drive to Brett's house? A car had followed me. Was it a neighbor? Someone who knew me?

"I'm—" My voice broke. "I'm here."

"Have you spoken with Jillian?" Nick asked. "Does she have any idea where Brett might be?"

I gulped hard and tried to steady my voice.

"No, Jillian doesn't know where he could be," I said, forcing my mind to work. "The detectives must have found something by now. They *must* have. Something had to have popped. There've been no hits on his credit cards? No cell phone calls? Nothing?"

"Not so far," he said. "Did Jillian mention anything she may have forgotten to tell the detectives?"

A knot of guilt twisted my stomach. I'd lied to Nick about being at the scene of the murder. If I was going to tell the truth, it had to be now, before I got any deeper into this investigation.

But I couldn't do it. I couldn't come forward now. If the cops were already focusing on Jillian, what would they do if they found out she'd lied to them about the night of the murder? They'd think she was lying about other things. It would only get worse for her.

And it wouldn't be so great for me, either.

I sure wished I could get a do-over on that decision.

"Look, I've got to get back to work," I said.

Nick didn't say anything. I didn't know if he was thinking, or if he was using his cop keep-quiet technique to force me to fill the silence and perhaps divulge something important. If that was his intent, I wasn't falling for it.

"Thanks for the heads-up on the investigation," I said.

Nick hadn't had to call and tell me those things, and he was probably taking a risk revealing information about an ongoing investigation.

"I appreciate it," I said. "Really."

He was quiet for a few seconds then said, "You're not involving yourself in this, are you, Dana?"

He didn't sound like a cop now. He sounded like a worried—friend, boyfriend? I didn't know.

"Just concerned about my friend," I said and tried to sound casual. I didn't think it came off that way.

"I have a customer waiting," I said.

I didn't feel so great about lying to get rid of him after he'd called to share important info with me, but what else could I do?

"Thanks again," I said.

We ended the call and I left the restroom with one thought pounding in my head: no matter what it took, I absolutely had to find Brett.

Dorothy Howell

# Chapter 7

I couldn't find Brett.

After spending the morning and most of the afternoon calling my customers for cover and jumping between data bases when no one was looking, I'd failed to come up with any current info about Brett Sinclair. And not only could I not find him, I couldn't find but the smallest trace of evidence that he even existed.

No wonder the detectives were having so much trouble locating him.

I'd pulled a credit bureau report and discovered he had two credit cards, both with zero balances, both opened within the last year. That was it. Very unusual for a man in his thirties.

The property search I'd done came up empty. Brett wasn't on the deed to any residential property in Santa Flores, or elsewhere in California. His house in Maywood must have been a rental. I found no record that Brett owned commercial property. Nick had been right. Brett managed—not owned—a restaurant somewhere. I wondered if I'd misunderstood what Brett had told me, or if he'd deliberately misled me.

I discovered a cell phone listed in his name. Tempted as I was to call the number, I didn't dare. The cops were monitoring it, surely, watching for any activity that might reveal Brett's location.

The only other info I'd found involved two checking accounts Brett had opened at banks here in Santa Flores. One was a joint account with Alexa; no big surprise there. The other was also a joint account, this one held with someone named Laurel Duncan. I had no idea who she was. A girlfriend? A business partner? His grandma? I needed to find out. Maybe Crystal would know.

I glanced at the wall clock above the filing cabinets and saw that it was getting close to three. I hadn't taken my lunch hour yet, so I shut down my computer and gathered my things.

"I'm heading out to Webster and pay a visit to that customer I mentioned this morning. I'll do it while I'm at lunch," I said to Manny as I stopped by his desk. He was on the phone so he just nodded.

From the corner of my eye I saw Inez watch me walk past her desk, look at the clock, then make a note on her calendar. I figured my timesheet would likely be a visual aid in her next office meeting. I could have mentioned that I was going on a field call and that I'd be gone for more than my lunch hour, but I wasn't feeling that generous at the moment, especially toward Inez.

I wanted to get to Quota Vino in time to catch Crystal before she started her shift and normally I would have walked there. But since I was supposedly going on a field call, I got in my car, drove a block over, and parked in a small lot behind the wine bar that was used by employees and delivery trucks.

Only a few vehicles were there, so I found a good spot where I could watch cars as they drove in. I also got a not-so-inviting view of the rear of the place—a Dumpster heaped with garbage, stacks of wooden crates and cardboard boxes surrounded by chunks of decaying vegetables, and more grime than anyone wants to see in close proximity to a place where they've actually eaten.

The back door was propped open and workers in soiled white aprons were coming and going, some to the Dumpster, others to what I guessed was an exterior storage room at the corner of the building. One of the cooks talked on his cell phone and puffed a cigarette as he paced.

I'd taken a chance that Crystal would show up for her shift today and I was relieved when a blue Chevy Malibu rolled into the lot and she got out. She was tall with dark hair, probably in her early thirties, and dressed in her waitress uniform of black pants and shirt.

Crystal shouldered a tote bag and locked her car. I intercepted her near the door of the restaurant.

"Hi, Crystal," I said, stepping in front of her.

She stopped, startled. A few seconds passed before I saw recognition bloom on her face.

"Oh, yeah, Dana," she said, then nodded toward the building. "The front entrance is for customers."

"I wanted to talk to you," I said.

She glanced at her watch and I knew she was worried about clocking-in late. I hurried on.

"I heard about what happened to Alexa Sinclair," I said and managed to sound troubled. "I was concerned because I've seen Brett here so often. Is it safe for me and my friends to still come here?"

I'd planned what to say on the way over. I hoped I'd pulled it off and she believed me.

She didn't seem to, so I pushed ahead.

"You know, do you think there's a connection between her death and Brett, maybe?" I asked.

"I've got no clue," Crystal said. "I haven't seen or heard from Brett, and the cops aren't saying anything."

"Oh," I said, hoping I sounded confused. "I thought you and Brett were close. You used to date, didn't you?"

Crystal rolled her eyes. "Nothing's a secret at this place, is it? Yes, we used to date. Yes, it was serious. Yes, we were talking about getting married. Until Princess Alexa came along, that is."

She didn't seem the least bit troubled about speaking ill of the dead, so I rolled with it.

"I heard she could be difficult," I said. It was a lie, but I wanted to keep her talking. "What did Brett see in her?"

"Her bank balance," Crystal said. "Or her daddy's bank balance, I should say. Alexa laid eyes on Brett and decided she wanted him. I know she tempted him with all that money her family had, and believe me, she didn't have much else going for her. Brett fell for it. You can't blame him. He's always involved in business deals and needs capital."

"You mean the restaurant?" I asked.

"Oh, yes, that place." Crystal shook her head. "He's partners with his sister. She runs it. Brett doesn't really have much to do with it. He can't be tied down with that sort of thing. He needs his freedom to work his other deals. All the good businessmen are like that."

"He takes half of the profits but lets his sister do all the work?" I asked.

Crystal's back stiffened. "It was Laurel's idea."

Laurel Duncan was the name I'd read on the checking account held jointly with Brett.

"Brett and Laurel are close?" I asked. "Sometimes brothers and sisters don't get along."

"Laurel idolizes Brett," Crystal said.

"She must be upset about Alexa's murder."

"Guess again," Crystal said with a bitter laugh. "Alexa was a princess. She never worked a day in her life and here's Laurel knocking herself out to try and keep that kid's café above water. Laurel couldn't stand her."

It sounded as if Crystal couldn't stand her, either, which didn't surprise me.

"They were separated, getting a divorce, you know," Crystal said. "Married less than a year, and she was out of there. What a princess. She didn't appreciate Brett. Not for one minute."

"Have you seen Brett since the murder?" I asked.

She'd told me already she hadn't, but I figured it couldn't hurt to ask again while her guard was down.

"Not yet." She glanced at her watch.

"Let me know if you hear from him, will you?" I asked, trying to sound concerned. "I'd like to give him my condolences."

"Sure. Look, I've got to go," she said, and cut around me heading for the employee entrance.

Flynn, the busser who'd knocked over my drink yesterday, stood in the doorway. He stepped aside to let her in.

How long had he been standing there? He had been eavesdropping on our conversation?

His gaze met and held mine. I turned away and got into my car. When I pulled out of the parking spot, Flynn was gone.

I swung around to the next row of parked cars and stopped behind Crystal's Chevy, then pulled out my cell phone and took a photo of her license plate. As I drove toward the exit I glanced at the employee entrance. Flynn was in the doorway again, watching me.

What was with that guy?

I pulled onto Fleming Avenue and headed for the freeway.

The lie I'd told Manny about wanting to field call an account in Webster would give me plenty of time to find Laurel Duncan. Crystal had said she and Brett were close, so she'd very likely know where to find him. I was sure the homicide detectives had already contacted her, but I doubted she'd ratted out her own brother.

At the next corner I stopped for the traffic light and Googled the description of Laurel's business that Crystal had mentioned. I found a place named Kidz Korner Kafé in Hayward, a town about twenty minutes or so east of Santa Flores. It was the only local business that even vaguely matched the description. I decided to give it a try.

Traffic moved forward. At the next red light I sent a text to Slade, along with the photo of Crystal's license plate, and asked if he could get me her address. The DMV database wasn't one I had access to at Mid-America but Slade had a contact there who could get me the information.

When the light changed I moved forward with the traffic, my conversation with Crystal playing in my head.

Had she really not heard from Brett? She obviously still had feelings for him. Were they strong enough that she'd lie for him? Probably.

Would she kill for him?

The idea flew into my head as I stopped at the next traffic light.

Crystal claimed Brett and Alexa were separated and a divorce was in the works. Did Crystal see that as the perfect opportunity to get back together with him? Had she not wanted to risk a reconciliation, taken matters into her own hands, and murdered Alexa?

If so, why had Crystal murdered Alexa on the night Jillian was at Brett's house?

It hit me that maybe Brett and Crystal had been in on the murder together. Maybe Jillian's presence was planned. Had they intended to use her, to make her look guilty? If so, it was working.

But only if Brett knew Alexa planned to come to the house that night, I realized, which was entirely possible. At this point, I had no way of knowing for sure.

All the more reason to find Brett.

I turned onto Third Street and cut over two lanes to catch the south bound freeway entrance, and spotted my brother standing on the sidewalk outside an insurance office.

"What the . . .?"

I hit the brakes and craned my neck to get a better look. A horn honked behind me. I kept staring.

It was definitely my brother. I thought I'd seen him yesterday but wasn't sure. Now I was positive it was him.

What was he doing in Santa Flores? Where was Denise? And why hadn't I heard from Mom about a family dinner she was having for them?

I whipped into the driveway of a dentist's office down the block and stopped, fished my cell phone from my handbag, and called him. I watched as he hung around the front of the insurance office, then pulled his phone from his pocket, looked at the ID screen, and answered.

"What's going on, Rob?" I asked.

I got a little tingle in my stomach. I was going to call him out about being in town and, finally, get the best of my big brother.

"Just working," he said.

"You're working? Really?" I said. "You sound like you're outside."

I was ready to blow my horn and wave so he'd see me, then yell "busted" and we'd have a laugh.

"Heading to a meeting in the next building," Rob said.

A little chill ran down my spine.

"So what's up?" he asked.

I was too stunned to speak.

"Dana?" he said.

"Yeah," I finally said. "When are you and Denise coming back to town?"

I watched as he paced, staring at the tips of his shoes.

"Who knows?" he said. "Maybe in a couple of—"

Rob looked up suddenly as a woman approached. She was tall, blonde, probably my age, and dressed in a navy blue business suit. She stopped next to him.

"Look, Dana," Rob said. "I've got to go. Meeting's starting. I'll talk to you later."

He ended the call.

I hit the gas and shot into the parking lot behind the dentist's office, looped around, and stopped in the driveway again. I looked down the block. No sign of Rob and the blonde woman.

Rob had lied. He'd lied about being in town. Why would he do that?

I sat there trying not to make a snap decision or rush to judgement about Rob and the woman. But I couldn't think of a reason—except the obvious one—why he'd be in town, hanging out with a woman who wasn't his wife, and lying about it.

Not long ago I'd gone through something similar with my mom and dad. I couldn't do that again.

I accessed the contact list on my phone and called Rob. My call went to voicemail.

I hung up, turned right onto Third Street, and headed for the freeway entrance.

# Chapter 8

I found a parking space just down the block from the Kidz Korner Kafé and got out. This area of Hayward had a quaint, English village look to it. All the businesses were small specialty shops painted in pastels, with flower boxes running over with blooming plants. The restaurants had cozy seating areas outside featuring wrought iron tables and colorful umbrellas.

The Kidz Korner Kafé was painted butter yellow. The big plate glass window was decorated with nursery rhyme characters. Stroller parking was available near the entrance.

I figured it was nap time when I walked in because the place was empty except for two young moms seated at a table in the corner, their sleeping infants in carriers next to them. Nearby was a play area filled with toys. Through open French doors I spotted a flower garden enclosed by a picket fence that held a sandbox, a baby swing, and tables and chairs.

The Kidz Korner Kafé might cater to children but it was designed for moms, I realized, after I glanced at the handwritten daily menu posted near the entrance that included wine by the glass.

A young woman walked out from what I figured was the kitchen, wearing a yellow apron with Mother Goose on the front. She was tall with blonde hair. I knew right away she was Laurel Duncan, Brett's sister. The family resemblance was uncanny. But where Brett always looked carefree, Laurel had a no-nonsense air about her, the kind of person you'd want on your team when a big project was due because you knew she'd do most of the work—and it would be right.

"Laurel?" I said as I approached her. I introduced myself and said, "Could I talk to you about Brett?"

She glanced at her two customers on the other side of the restaurant, then turned to me and lowered her voice. "If you're a reporter, or something, you can leave right now."

I knew there was no point in trying to pull off anything deceptive with her, so I went with the truth.

"My friend is a suspect in Alexa's death," I said, even though it was stretching the truth a bit. "She's innocent but the police are giving her a hard time. She was with Brett the night Alexa was murdered. I need to find him so he can tell them she's not involved."

Laurel uttered a disgusted grunt and glanced away, then looked at me again and sighed.

"Come on," she said, and led the way out the front entrance. We stopped near the stroller parking area and she went on. "Look, I don't know where Brett is. The police were already here and I told them the same thing."

"You must be worried about him," I said.

"I'm worried that Alexa's murder will ruin my business. It's a café that caters to moms with little kids. Do you think they'll come around once word gets out? This place is one bad week away from going under." Laurel shook her head. "Something else Brett will likely screw up for me."

"I've got a brother, too," I said. Rob wasn't a screw-up but I hoped that if we found some common ground, she'd keep talking. "You two own the business together?"

"Only because I couldn't swing it any other way," Laurel said. "Mom and Dad left everything to the both of us. Fifty-fifty, right down the middle. I needed Brett's money to get the place up and running, so Brett is a partner, technically, but I want him as far away from here as possible."

"But that leaves you doing all the work," I said.

"Which suits me fine," Laurel said. "Mr. Entrepreneur. Always with a big business deal in the works. One time he showed up here with some guy telling me about a garage he was investing in. The guy looked shady, like most of Brett's so-called business associates. I told them to leave."

"Did Alexa know about Brett's questionable investments?" I asked.

"I doubt it occurred to her to ask—before the wedding." Laurel shrugged. "But she must have figured out pretty quickly that something was wrong."

"I heard they were separated, getting a divorce," I said.

"He claimed she was having an affair. Who knows? Alexa did to suit herself." Laurel glanced inside the café and said, "I've got to go."

She disappeared inside and I headed back to my car.

I'd wondered if Crystal had murdered Alexa. Now I wondered if Laurel had done it, but for a different reason.

With Alexa and Brett divorcing, Laurel's café could be jeopardized. He was her partner in the place, so she could possibly lose out in the settlement.

Had Laurel killed Alexa to put a stop to the divorce and insure her own financial security?

I clicked the locks on my Honda and got inside.

Laurel didn't seem like the murdering type, but she'd obviously had it with her brother. She was in dire straits, financially. Plus, Crystal had said Laurel had never liked Alexa. Could those things have pushed Laurel over the edge, turned her into a murderer?

Possibly.

In my search for Brett earlier today I hadn't found much to go on. But Laurel had told me he had an interest in a garage somewhere, and that meant he had money and was, obviously, hiding it. A good attorney would find it, meaning Brett would likely lose at least half of it and probably the garage, too.

The divorce was a great reason for Brett to murder Alexa. What better way to get out of a property settlement, financial loss— and avoid his sister's wrath.

I started my car and pulled out into traffic.

Brett was the obvious suspect in Alexa's murder, as I saw it. Both Crystal and Laurel were potential suspects as well. Why were the cops focusing on Jillian?

I was going to have to talk to Nick again.

\*\*\*

My spirits fell when I pulled into the Mid-America parking lot and saw that Mr. Frazier's green Buick was still there. I'd hoped he'd concluded his office visit while I was in Hayward on my supposed field call and he'd headed out already or, since it was almost five o'clock, he'd left early. No such luck.

Inside, Carmen wore a grim expression when I walked past the front counter. Jade and Manny had their heads down, working. There was no sign of Inez and Mr. Burrows' office door was closed.

"What did I miss?" I whispered to Manny when I stopped at his desk.

"Mr. Burrows pulled Inez into his office. All three of them are in there," he said in a low voice

A number of scenarios collided in my head—none of them good.

"They're probably telling Inez about Burrows' retirement, since she's under him," Manny said. "And, our new employee is in there, too."

"We have a new finance rep?" I asked.

"I don't think so." Manny shook his head. "She hasn't been introduced to the staff yet, but she looks like one of those hot shots Corporate lured away from another company and put on the fast track for a management position with us."

Mental alarm bells went off in my head.

"This new person is going to be our manager?" I asked, and heard the rising panic in my voice.

A manager who'd never worked for Mid-America was the worst possible thing that could happen to our branch. Everyone would expect her to come out of the gate posting stellar results, which any normal person knew wasn't possible with her lack of knowledge and experience operating under Mid-America policies. She would feel the pressure to perform and would attempt to do so by leaning heavily on all the employees and causing us to do our work along with a portion of hers.

As if that possibility wasn't awful enough, another idea bloomed in my head, causing a sick feeling to sweep over me.

"You don't think they're going to promote Inez to branch manager, do you?" I asked.

"Holy crap," Manny moaned. "I hope not."

My possible job in Pasadena was looking better by the moment.

"Maybe they'll make Inez the interim manager until this new hire can take over," Manny said.

"There's no way I can work for Inez," I told Manny.

Of course, making my resignation Inez's first official act as branch manager might make it worthwhile.

We both stewed on those dreadful scenarios for a minute, then Manny changed the subject.

"What happened on your field call? Catch them at home?" he asked, shuffling papers across his desk.

It took me a few seconds to remember I'd made up that

excuse to get out of the office.

"No. Nobody was home," I told him. The lie came out easily enough but I hurried to my desk before he could ask anything else.

I had about a half hour to kill before I could leave, and because Mr. Frazier and the new hire who might end up being my boss were here, I spent the time working. I pulled up my phone route and went through the motions of calling customers, but my thoughts were stretched in too many directions to be very effective.

Turmoil in the office. My brother in town secretly and hanging out with an attractive young woman. Nick back in my life. That new job possibility in Pasadena.

Where was my best friend when I needed to talk?

No way could I call Jillian and discuss my problems, not when she was buried under a massive situation herself. But I really could use another ear to listen to everything, or maybe a shoulder to lean on.

Nick flew into my head. For a few moments I let the image of him fill my thoughts and I envisioned myself pouring out my problems, him listening patiently, putting his arm around me, pulling me against his chest, and whispering that everything would be all right. Somehow, when Nick said those few words, it made me believe that everything really would be all right.

Except that I couldn't talk to him about anything personal.

But I could ask him about the Alexa Sinclair murder investigation. I needed to find out what was going on and why the detectives assigned to the case were ignoring Brett, Crystal, and Laurel as suspects and aiming their investigation at Jillian. Something must have come up that I didn't know about. Maybe Nick knew and would fill me in.

I picked up my cell phone, intending to go to the restroom and call Nick, then thought better of it. Right now I was wound up, stressed out, and a knot of nerves ready to explode. If I heard Nick's voice, I might lose it.

Not the best way to meet the new hire or face Mr. Frazier.

The door to Mr. Burrows' office opened. Inez was the first one out, followed by the woman who might become our branch manager. Mr. Frazier was on her heels. Mr. Burrows straggled behind, looking none too happy.

Manny and I exchanged a troubled glance.

---

"Attention! Attention in the office!" Inez called out, as if everyone hadn't already turned to stare.

"This is Sasha Vaughn," Mr. Frazier said in a tone that indicated this was a done deal and we were all just going to have to live with it.

I figured she was about my age, maybe a year or two older, tall and shapely, and dressed in a business suit that could have been a designer label. Her makeup was perfect and her red hair was twisted into a chic chignon.

Mr. Frazier made introductions by telling Sasha our names and positions in the branch. Manny got up from his desk and shook her hand. Carmen, Jade, and I waved.

"Sasha comes to us from Greater Inland Mortgage right here in Santa Flores," Mr. Frazier said.

Manny had been right. Sasha was a big gun hired away from another company. She looked the part. The finance reps we usually hired were young, just starting out in the business world. Sasha had an air about her that said she was burning her way up the corporate ladder and this particular rung was a temporary stop.

"Sasha will be working here," Mr. Frazier told us.

I had questions about what Sasha's presence in our branch really meant, but no more information was forthcoming. She managed a smile that indicated she could look pleasant when necessary, then spoke to Mr. Frazier in a low voice. He nodded and she left the office, not giving any of us a second look as she walked out the front door.

"We have seven more minutes," Inez called out, gesturing to the wall clock. "Let's make them count."

Good grief.

Mr. Frazier made a few remarks to Mr. Burrows, then left the office while we all pretended to work. Mr. Burrows ducked into his own office and closed the door. I shut down my computer, gathered my things and left, rebel that I am, even though two full minutes remained in the work day. Inez would likely have said something as I walked past her desk but she was busy typing, probably an agenda for an upcoming office meeting where she would tell us everything we already knew.

I jumped in my Honda and swung out onto Fifth Street, then turned onto Fleming Avenue heading for the freeway entrance. Up ahead I spotted that hideous green Buick that Mr. Frazier drove as he turned into the parking lot of the Santa Flores Inn, an upscale boutique hotel. I'd been inside once tracking down one of my customers who worked there and was behind on his account with us. I knew the place was gorgeous and expensive. Mid-America must have treated Mr. Frazier to a very lenient expense account.

I hit the freeway and drove to my apartment. The security lighting had come on by the time I swung into a parking space. When I got out of my car the image of Nick flared in my head. I needed to call him and find out what, exactly, was happening with the murder investigation. I'd have to contact Jillian and let her know. Maybe I'd go over to her place tonight.

I crossed the parking lot and headed up the sidewalk toward the stairs that led to my apartment formulating a quick plan—change into comfy jeans and T-shirt, eat the leftover pot roast my mom had sent home with me on Sunday, then try to reach Nick and—

"Dana?" a male voice called from the shadows.

I jumped and my heart rate shot up. Nick? Had he come to see me? Was he here to tell me things had gotten worse for Jillian in the investigation? Or would he—finally—explain why I hadn't heard from him in months, apologize, and tell me he couldn't live without me a moment longer?

He stepped closer and my heart rate amped up higher.

This guy wasn't Nick. He was a little taller than me, slender, wearing jeans and a hooded jacket. He turned so the security lighting caught his face.

"Flynn?" I asked.

I couldn't seem to process what was happening. Why was the busser from Quota Vino outside my apartment building?

"You startled me," I said. "What are you doing here?"

Flynn nodded toward the buildings across the courtyard from mine.

"I live here," he said.

The complex was huge and spread out over several acres, with multiple entrances and exits. It wasn't hard to believe he lived here and I'd never seen him.

"Is Jillian all right? The cops are trying to pin this on her, aren't they?" Flynn said. "Is she okay?"

I didn't think Jillian would want me sharing a lot of her personal information that would likely get passed around at Quota Vino, so I said, "She's good."

"That's it? That's all you got?" he asked, and took a step closer. "You're supposed to be her friend. Don't you know how she's doing?"

I was more than a little annoyed at this point.

"Look, Flynn, don't come around here jumping out at me in the dark," I told him. "When I see Jillian again and find out how she's doing, I'll let everyone at Quota Vino know."

"Jillian deserves better than you," Flynn murmured.

He cut around me, coming so close his sleeve brushed my arm. I whirled and watched as he disappeared around the building.

All I wanted at that moment was to be safe and sound inside my apartment. I dashed up the stairs and into the interior hallway.

Nick waited outside my door.

## Chapter 9

I wasn't sure if I was relieved or annoyed at seeing Nick.

Maybe a little of both.

His collar stood open and his necktie was pulled down, indicating he'd either had a rough day or he felt comfortable enough around me to loosen up a bit.

"Hungry?" Nick held up a takeout bag from my favorite Chinese restaurant.

"What are you doing here?" I asked.

"You want to talk about the investigation, don't you?" He rattled the bag. "Avocado egg rolls. Your favorite."

They were definitely a favorite of mine.

"Although I don't think they really have them in China," Nick said, and gave me one of his infamous grins.

I couldn't resist either one.

"No dessert?" I asked as I unlocked the door.

"We can improvise," he whispered from behind me.

The heat from his body radiated over me and his warm breath brushed my cheek. I lingered for a few seconds, then forced myself to open the door and go into my apartment.

I flipped on the lights in the entryway as Seven Eleven trotted out from the kitchen. Traitor that she was, she ignored me and wound herself between Nick's ankles.

"Go change," he told me. "Get comfortable."

As I headed down the hallway I heard him pop the lid on a can of cat food, and Seven Eleven meowing her little head off.

In my bedroom I wasn't sure what level of *get comfortable* I should go for. I didn't want to give Nick any ideas—well, at least none of the ideas that were exploding in *my* head—by slipping into a silk bathrobe and leaving my hair loose around my shoulders. Yet I couldn't bring myself to smear my face with heavy duty night cream, wrap my hair in a towel, and put on a ratty old sweatshirt and stretched-out yoga pants. I settled for jeans and a white T-shirt, and put my hair in a ponytail.

As I headed for the kitchen I passed through the living room, opened the drapes, and cracked open the sliding glass door that led to my balcony. I'd bought a tri-level cat perch and scratching post for Seven Eleven as a Christmas gift—not that I'd been lonely or anything—and put it out there for her so she could get some fresh air.

I'd worried about her falling over the railing, but she was very surefooted and not particularly adventuresome. I sat out there with her most of the time. My patio overlooked one of the complex's greenbelts and the adjoining vacant lot, rather than another apartment building, so the view was nice for both of us.

When I went to the kitchen, Nick had hung his sport coat and shoulder holster on the back of a chair and was sipping a Corona from my refrigerator. He'd put plates, forks, and napkins on the table along with the little cartons of takeout. Seven Eleven chowed down at her bowl in the corner.

Nick passed me a beer and we settled into chairs across from each other at the table.

"What's been going on lately?" Nick asked as we filled our plates.

I didn't know exactly how far back *lately* should go. All the way to last November when we'd last spoken? Should I mention how lonely and upset I'd been? How I was so desperate to get away I'd applied for a new job in Pasadena? And it was all because of him?

The incident back in high school with Nick and my best friend Katie Jo Miller—rumors that he's the one who'd gotten her pregnant, made her have an abortion, then dumped her and left town—popped into my head. Even though the matter had been settled, it somehow lingered between us. I was sure Nick didn't want to talk about it. I certainly didn't.

I opted for pleasant dinner conversation.

"I've been working, mostly," I said. "We've got a new person in our office. Somebody from a mortgage company here in town. She just showed up today."

Nick nodded as he bit into an egg roll. "The branch has been short-handed since around Christmas, hasn't it?"

"How did you know?" I asked.

"I know lots of things, Dana," he told me, in a way that made me think he'd intended some deeper meaning. He went on before I could ask and said, "I'm thinking about buying a new car."

We talked about cars for a while—he wanted another Camaro, or maybe a Corvette, and I was thinking of upgrading my Honda to a BMW one of these days—and the conversation meandered from one noncontroversial topic to another. Seven Eleven finished her dinner and curled up at Nick's feet to groom herself. I relaxed, more contented than I'd felt in a while.

"How's Jillian holding up?" Nick asked as he sat back and pushed his empty plate away.

"Not so good," I told him.

He seemed to brace himself, preparing for the inevitable. But that's why he'd come here tonight, wasn't it? To discuss the investigation?

It occurred to me then that perhaps there was more to this visit. He had bad news and wanted to break it to me personally?

My anxiety level amped up. I slid my plate to the side.

"Brett Sinclair is still missing," Nick said. "There's no trace of him. Cell phone, credit cards, bank account all show nothing. No activity of any sort. Absolutely nothing."

"He couldn't have just disappeared," I said. "Nobody just vanishes. There must be some trace of him somewhere."

"No sign of his car," Nick said. "None of his relatives or friends has heard from him."

"What about his partner at the garage in Devon?" I asked. "He must know something. Did you talk to him?"

Nick's brows drew together. "How did you know about that auto repair business?"

Since I'd told Nick I wasn't involved in the case, I couldn't tell him the truth about how I'd found out.

I gave him what I hoped was a thoughtful look and said, "It must have been from Brett. He talked about himself all the time. He must have mentioned it one night at Quota Vino."

Nick's brows unfurled slightly so I went on.

"Brett, obviously, planned this whole thing. He got a fake ID. He squirreled away cash. He got a burner phone and a different car," I said. "This proves he murdered Alexa."

Nick shook his head, unconvinced.

I pushed on. "It was an elaborate setup to implicate Jillian. She's just a pawn in this sick game of his to get rid of his wife."

He shook his head again.

"There must be other suspects," I insisted. "What about the employees at Quota Vino? Brett was always in there. He was a regular. Maybe he was a crappy tipper. Maybe someone there had a grudge against him? Do any of them have criminal records?"

I hoped he'd tell me that Crystal was a person of interest, as I'd suspected. She certainly had a motive.

"Nothing of any consequence," Nick said.

My spirits lifted. "So somebody who works there has a record?"

"Domestic violence," he told me. "But that was nearly fifteen years ago, and nothing since."

"It was Gabe, wasn't it?" I said, since he was the only person I'd seen in Quota Vino who appeared to be the right age.

Nick didn't answer my question, so I figured I'd guessed correctly.

"Some juvenile stuff," he said. "Nothing serious."

"Who?" I asked.

Nick didn't look as if he intended to divulge that information, so I took another guess.

"It was that guy Flynn, wasn't it?" I said. "He's kind of creepy now, so he must have been a creepy kid."

Nick paused for a moment and said, "An unidentified fingerprint was found inside the house."

My breath caught. Could the fingerprint be mine? Is that what Nick had come to tell me? That I was going to be brought in for questioning? Was he going to take me in himself? Now?

My thoughts raced back over the events of that night. After I arrived at the house, what had I touched? I'd been in the kitchen, the dining room, and the entryway. I'd bumped into the china hutch. Had I touched something else? A door frame? The kitchen counter?

Then it hit me. I'd rung the doorbell. My entire thumb print was on the ringer button.

"It appears that somebody else was in the house," Nick said.

It took all my emotional, mental, and physical strength not to bolt from the chair.

"It could have been anybody," I said, and struggled to speak slowly and sound reasonable. "Really, anybody. You know, somebody who had nothing to do with the murder."

"We're checking the prints of the housekeeper, the gardener, the service people who'd been there recently," Nick said. "We'll find out who it is."

"That's a waste of time," I insisted. "You shouldn't spend resources on a lead that will go nowhere. Trace Brett's activities. Find out where he bought a burner phone. See if he withdrew a large amount of cash from the bank over the past several months. Look for a recent car title transfer at the DMV."

Nick's brows drew together again and I knew I sounded like a crazy person. Hopefully not a guilty crazy person.

I sat back. "Okay, I know I'm getting carried away. I'm just concerned about Jillian. That's all."

"I'm concerned, too," Nick said. He paused for a few seconds and said, "You know, Dana, you have to consider the possibility that Jillian is guilty, that she killed Alexa."

Before I could voice my protest, Nick went on.

"And with Brett missing," he said, "there's a good chance Jillian murdered him, too."

So that's why Nick came over. To tell me in person that the homicide detectives thought she was a double murderer. No wonder they were focusing their investigation on her.

I couldn't bear the thought.

"Ridiculous," I said and hopped out of the chair.

I opened a cupboard door and grabbed a plastic container for the leftovers. When I turned back, Nick was standing. I couldn't bring myself to meet his gaze. His cop x-ray vision had a way of penetrating my defenses and causing me to blurt out things I didn't want to say.

All I could think was what a terrible friend I'd been to abandon Jillian at Brett's house that night. If I'd stayed there, if two of us had related the same story, if I'd told the detectives about my connection to Nick, perhaps things wouldn't have gone this far. Maybe Jillian wouldn't be in this mess right now.

This was all my fault.

"You're upset," Nick said. "This isn't solely about Jillian being questioned in a murder investigation. Something else is going on with you."

I raked the leftover fried rice into the plastic contained.

"I can't fix it if I don't know what's wrong," he said.

His voice was soft and mellow, rich with concern and understanding that made me yearn to melt into him, confess everything, let him help me unload my burdensome guilty conscience. I wanted to. I really wanted to.

Yet I didn't dare.

I snapped the lid on the plastic container and said, "Did you eat enough? Do you want anything else?"

"How about dessert?" Nick said.

He reached around me. I thought he was going for the last egg roll but he caught my shoulder and lowered his head. He kissed me. I rose on my toes and kissed him back. He encircled me with his arms and pulled me against him. I looped my arms around his neck and held on. It was one of those long, slow kisses that builds, and just when I thought we might sprawl across my kitchen table and send the leftovers flying, I came to my senses.

I pulled back.

"This would only complicate things," I said.

"This isn't complicated," he told me.

Going further wouldn't resolve anything, only make the situation more difficult, for me, anyway. I tried to say that, to explain, but no words came out. All I managed was a slight shrug.

Nick got the message.

He stepped away. He made quick work of tossing the trash and putting our dishes in the sink, then slipped his shoulder holster in place and picked up his sport coat.

I walked with him to the door. He stepped into the hallway and turned back. I didn't want him to go, but I couldn't ask him to stay when so many things between us were unresolved.

I realized then how much I wanted our situation to improve. Yet that would only happen if one of us tried to make it so.

I took a chance.

"Why haven't you contacted me since last November?" I asked.

Nick grinned. "I'm here now. Isn't that what matters?"

"That's not an answer."

He sighed. His shoulders slumped and he shook his head. "Can't you ever let things go, Dana? Do you always have to drag up the past and rehash things that are over and done with?"

"Maybe I could," I said, "if I knew exactly what I was dealing with and had some assurance the problems from the past wouldn't happen again."

"You need to learn to get over things," he told me.

"I never *get over* anything," I said. "You're just going to

---

have to learn to live with it."

He didn't respond.

"Or not," I said.

Nick gave me a sharp look, then nodded.

"Lock up," he said.

I closed the door and slid the dead bolt into place. Even though I didn't want to, I put my eye to the peep hole and looked out.

Nick wasn't there.

Dorothy Howell

## Chapter 10

I arrived at the office the next morning a full two minutes before Mid-America's official start time and found Mr. Burrows' door closed. Inez wasn't at her desk. Something was up. No way would Inez be late for work.

I stowed my handbag in my desk drawer, grabbed a file folder for cover, and joined Manny at the copy machine.

"What's going on?" I whispered.

Manny glanced at Sasha seated at the desk our previous finance rep had occupied and gave me a meaningful eyebrow bob. I returned the bob. We both knew we had a likely spy in our midst and we had to be careful what we said.

"Inez got pulled into Mr. Burrows' office as soon as she walked in," Manny murmured. "Mr. Frazier's in there, too. They're probably telling her that Burrows is retiring."

My spirits fell.

"So we'll end up with either Inez or Sasha as our new branch manager?" I asked.

"It could happen," he said.

"Inez would make us all crazy," I said, then threw a quick glance at Sasha. "And what about her? Does she have management experience? She's been working at a mortgage company. Yeah, it's local, so she knows the area. But what did she do there? Is she really up for managing our branch?"

Manny shrugged. He didn't know the answers to my questions and even if he did, it wouldn't matter. Mid-America routinely hired supposed hot shot employees from other companies and brought them on board knowing they weren't qualified to run one of our branches. Upper management had a training program, which amounted to a procedures manual for them to read, and counted on the branch employees to take up the slack training-wise. There were always lots of candidates for Mid-America to choose from since our company paid higher salaries than banks and mortgage companies, plus offered monthly bonuses and other perks.

Never mind that we employees, who were doing most of the

work, got none of those benefits.

Noise at the front of the office drew my attention. Carmen came into the branch, followed a few seconds later by Jade.

"Morning," Carmen called with a bright smile.

Sasha didn't look up. I'd walked in ready to display a pleasant expression for her benefit, but she hadn't acknowledged me. She either had her game face on or was simply being a bitch.

I went to my desk and got busy calling customers about their payments. Month-end was approaching and my figures were good, as always. I didn't have to work very hard today, I just had to *look* like that's what I was doing.

A few minutes later Inez walked out of Mr. Burrows' office. It wasn't like her to wear a sunny smile, but she looked positively grim. Apparently, she hadn't liked what Mr. Frazier had told her. She dropped into her desk chair and got to work.

Just when the tension in the office seemed unbearable, a wave of swishing blonde hair caught my eye. Jade rose from her desk.

I spotted Slade looking incredibly hot in jeans and a black T-shirt as he walked into the office.

"Good morning," Jade cooed.

"Hey," Slade said, then swung his gaze my way.

I was out of my chair and around the front counter before Jade could get her golden locks swept to her other shoulder. I blasted past her and out the front door, Slade on my heels.

"What's up?" I asked, as we stopped at the corner of the building.

I hadn't expected him to come by today. I didn't have any repo order out with Quality Recovery, and I hadn't heard from our Sacramento branch about the vehicle Slade had picked up for them earlier in the week.

"Break-in at the yard last night," Slade said.

I was surprised and concerned. Quality Recovery's lot was a fortress, surrounded by tall fences topped with razor wire and patrolled by a couple of big German shepherds.

"Are the dogs okay?" I asked.

Slade nodded. "They're good."

"What happened?"

"Kids," he said. "The dogs cornered them until the night guy got there."

"Did the police come?"

"Nah. No need." Slade grinned. "They won't come back."

I'd seen their night watchman, a hulk covered in leather and tats. Between him and the dogs, I figured Quality Recover was the last place those kids would ever go again.

"I'm guessing they damaged some of the cars," I said, since I couldn't imagine Slade would come here just to chat about vandalism.

"They dented hoods on a few cars trying to get away from the dogs. One was yours," Slade said. "Sorry."

"No big deal," I said. I was relieved this wasn't my problem to handle. "I'll pass it along to our Sacramento branch and let them decide what to do."

We were quiet for a while. Making conversation with Slade wasn't always easy, but since it didn't seem to bother him, I was okay with it, too. Besides, it kept me out of the office a while longer.

"How's Jillian?" Slade asked.

"Hanging in there, but just barely," I said, then remembered the last time I'd spoken with Slade about Alexa's murder and the questions I had for him.

"Where do you know Brett from?" I asked.

He paused for a moment then said, "Around."

I knew he didn't mean the wine bar or the kids' café. I got the feeling he was trying to avoid answering my question, perhaps to protect me from something—which I appreciated, but didn't find helpful.

"The homicide detectives are convinced Jillian killed Alexa," I said. "They think she killed Brett, too, since they can't find any trace of him."

Slade didn't respond, just looked at me.

I could see he was going to need more convincing to give up the info.

"It's nonsense," I told him. "Jillian wouldn't kill anybody. It's obvious that Brett did it and is hiding out somewhere."

The office door opened and Mr. Frazier walked out heading for lunch, I supposed. He was on his cell phone and didn't seem to notice me standing there with Slade. He got into his Buick and drove out of the parking lot.

"The cops are looking for him?" Slade asked.

"Not very hard, since they've pretty much decided Jillian is guilty," I said. "I've got to find Brett. It's the only way I can prove she had nothing to do with Alexa's murder."

"Is that what this is about?" he asked.

Slade pulled a slip of paper from the pocket of his jeans and handed it to me. On it was written Crystal's name and her home address.

"Your DMV contact came through," I said. "Thanks."

"Who is she?" Slade asked.

"Brett's ex-girlfriend," I said. "She's still crazy about him. She'd take him in, if he showed up at her place."

The office door opened again and Sasha walked out, sliding sunglasses on. She didn't acknowledge Slade and me, just got into a cherry red Lexus and pulled onto Fifth Street.

"Stay clear of this one," Slade told me. "Brett Sinclair is trouble."

He'd told me something like the before but, honestly, I didn't see how it was possible. Brett hung out at a wine bar. How much of a bad-ass could he be?

"Where's the garage he's involved with?" I asked.

Slade shook his head.

"I have to find him," I said. "I'm not going to confront him. I'm just going to snap a couple of pictures so I can prove to the cops he's still alive and Jillian didn't kill him. I'll follow him and see where he's staying. I'll go straight to the police and let them know so they can pick him up and put an end to this mess."

Slade studied me. I could almost see his mind working, deciding whether or not to share the info with me. It didn't look promising.

There was nothing left to do but confess.

"Okay, look, I screwed up," I told Slade. "Yes, Jillian put herself in that position by going to Brett's place, but I'm the reason the whole thing has spun completely out of control. It's my fault. Please, just tell me the name of the garage. She's my best friend. I've got to make this right."

I guess I'd finally said something Slade could identify with.

"Pro Auto Repair in Devon," he told me. "But you're not going there alone. I'm coming with you. Understand?"

"Yeah, sure, no problem," I said.

"Tomorrow night."

Slade walked away. I went back into the office.

\* \* \*

The mood in the office was tense all day. Inez hadn't said a word since coming out of Mr. Burrows' office this morning and she hadn't even checked the wall clock when any of us took our lunch break. Sasha had been on the computer at the desk next to Inez's doing who-knows-what, and trying to look important by continually going in and out of Mr. Burrows' office, where he and Mr. Frazier had been holed up all day. Carmen had been forcefully cheerful and Jade had spent even more time than usual flipping her hair around. Perspiration had glistened on Manny's brow all day; I thought he might stroke out at any moment.

I'd spent my time calling my customers, notating their accounts, getting their payments set to arrive in our office prior to the last day of the month. The month-end figures, for both lending and collecting, were what mattered. Bonuses were awarded and careers were ended based on those stats.

Things were shaping up nicely for me, collection-wise. I was on track to turn in great results, as usual. With everything else that was going on, I was relieved I didn't have any difficult customers to deal with.

Also, I didn't have to feel guilty about taking care of some personal business on company time. I checked out Crystal's home address that Slade had gotten for me. It was a small house in a so-so neighborhood not far from Quota Vino. If Brett was hiding there I'd have to do surveillance twenty-four-seven to find out, which wasn't possible. I'd have a better chance of getting info at the repair shop.

Even though I wasn't meeting Slade until tomorrow night, I wanted to check out Pro Auto Repair and gather some advance intel. I glanced around the office and saw that everyone was occupied, then did an internet search. I figured they'd have a website but nothing popped. I checked review sites for Santa Flores and finally found something, a dozen or so reviews that had been posted over a year ago.

I wondered how much repairing was actually going on at Pro Auto Repair.

Was this yet another business that Brett had invested in that was struggling, like the kids' café? Was he just bad at picking ventures or was Brett's involvement the kiss of death that drove a company into the ground?

Of course, the location of Pro Auto Repair probably wasn't helping, I realized when I read their address. They were situated on White Avenue, a couple of blocks off of State Street in Devon.

Devon, which adjoined Santa Flores on the northwest side of the city, had been a nice area once upon a time. Over the past several decades the homes had decayed, property values had fallen, gangs had brought in drugs and violence. Yet a lot of older, lifetime residents had hung on. I figured Pro Auto Repair was probably one of those family owned establishments that didn't want—or couldn't afford—to relocate, and relied on word of mouth and long-time customers to keep the business going.

Even though Devon wasn't the greatest neighborhood and could be dangerous, I didn't think it was bad enough for Slade to warn me away and insist on accompanying me tomorrow night. A lot of my Mid-America customers lived there. I'd traveled those streets and been into homes there many times.

"I need to cover a few things with you—Dana, is it?"

I collapsed the screen and looked up in one well-practiced motion, and saw Sasha in front of my desk. She had on a black business suit that looked as expensive as the one she'd worn yesterday. Her hair was once again in a conservative up-do. Those were the only pleasant looking things about her, including her expression.

Her sudden, sneak appearance at my desk combined with her apparent inability to have learned my name didn't sit well with me. Still, since I might end up working for her, I managed not to call her out on those things.

"I've been reviewing the branch's delinquent accounts and your collection efforts," Sasha told me.

So that's what she'd been doing all day. I relaxed, glad I'd held my tongue. My collections statistics were stellar month after month. Obviously, she was here to compliment me on them.

Maybe working for her wouldn't be so bad.

"I see room for a great deal of improvement," Sasha told me.

I just looked at her, wondering if I'd misunderstood.

"You need to work these accounts much harder," she went on.

"My figures are among the best in the division," I told her.

Sasha managed an indulgent, pitying smile and said, "Month-end figures are not necessarily an indication that a thorough job is being done."

My blood started to boil.

"I'm doing a thorough job," I told her.

"Yes, I'm sure you think you are," Sasha said.

I glanced in Manny's direction. He was the collection manager, my supervisor. He always spoke up for me, took my side, and kept me from going off on somebody in these situations. His desk was empty. Obviously, Sasha had planned her attack on me when Manny wasn't around.

"It's time you got serious about your job. I want to see more legal action taken against customers. More repossessions. More wage attachments." Sasha dropped the printout on my desk that she'd brought with her. "I've reviewed these accounts. Start with them. Get back with me on your progress."

Sasha walked away.

I nearly went over the desk after her.

Seething, I sat there trying not to explode. What nerve. Who did she think she was? Yeah, she might take over the branch but right now she had no authority to do anything. She was way out of line instituting changes, bypassing Manny, and dictating how I should do my job.

Then I remembered how she'd been in and out of Mr. Burrows' office all day. Had she been ratting me out to him and the DM? Did they have her back on these changes?

Just as I drew a breath trying to calm myself, I glanced down at the printout she'd given me and read the names of my customers she wanted me to crack down on. My anger shot up again.

These weren't just any customers. These were people who'd fallen on hard times through no fault of their own. I'd worked with them for months while they struggled to get their financial lives back on track. And Sasha expected me to start legal proceedings against them? Repossess our collateral?

I couldn't do it.

Where was Manny? I had to talk to him.

He still wasn't at his desk so I figured he was either in the breakroom or the restroom. I headed that way and found him guzzling a soda by the refrigerator, staring into space.

"You're not going to believe what Sasha just told me," I

hissed, and relayed the conversation. "I've been working with these customers for months. They're good people. They're trying really hard to get caught up. I can't suddenly turn on them like Sasha expects me do to."

Manny chugged his soda. I could see his stress level escalate with every word I spoke, which didn't make me feel so great about unloading on him.

I drew in a calming breath and said, "I'll put this aside for now. We can talk about it later."

He looked grateful, then grabbed another soda from the refrigerator and cracked it open. I went back to my desk.

The afternoon dragged by. I was in a crabby mood the entire time. My run-in with Sasha was bad enough, but on top of that was the fact that I hadn't been able to turn to Manny to fix my problem. Plus, my customers that I cared about were likely going to be put in very difficult positions. And as if that weren't enough, my best friend was a suspect in two murders, my brother was lying to me and obviously up to no-good, and Nick was still dodging my questions about things that were important to me.

Nick.

My anger spiked when I thought about how he'd been at my apartment last night, how I'd asked why he hadn't contacted me since November, and how he'd shrugged off my question without answering it. Then he'd had the gall—*the gall*—to suggest that spending the night wouldn't complicate things.

The vision of rolling around in bed with Nick flew into my head—and made me even angrier, this time at myself for having conjured up the image in the first place.

Commotion at the front of the office drew my attention. Carmen and Jade had their handbags and were heading for the door. I'd been so worked up I hadn't realized it was closing time.

I logged off my computer, grabbed my things, and shot through the office toward the entrance. To my surprise, Inez beat me to the door. I couldn't remember one single time when she wasn't the last to leave. Something wasn't right. She hadn't been herself all day.

"Inez?" I called as I followed her across the parking lot.

She kept walking. I was sure she'd heard me—she hears everything that goes on in the office—but she didn't stop.

I caught up with her at the door of her white Saturn.

"Are you okay?" I asked.

She kept her back to me and fumbled with her keys.

"Inez?" I said. "Inez!"

She turned to me. Tears stood in her eyes.

"Oh my God, Inez, what's wrong?" I blurted out.

"It's nothing," she insisted, blinking hard. "Everything's all right. Really. It's ... it's all right."

"No, it's not," I insisted. "What's going on?"

Her gaze darted across the parking lot. I spotted Sasha getting into her Lexus. She didn't wave or smile, just ignored us.

We waited until she backed out of the spot and turned onto Fifth Street.

"You're upset. Something happened," I said. "Does this have anything to do with your meeting this morning with Mr. Burrows and the DM?"

Inez sniffed and swallowed hard. "Yes. But it's all right. I understand completely. If the corporate office thinks I should retire, then so be it."

"What?" I asked. "Corporate wants *you* to retire?"

Manny and I had speculated that Mr. Burrows would get the axe. Had we been off base, or what?

"It's for the best," Inez said, drawing herself up straighter. "Sasha will make a fine replacement."

I gasped.

"You're being forced to retire so Sasha can have your job?" I asked.

Inez nodded. "I expect it's only temporary. She'll move up to branch manager soon."

No. No, no, no. This couldn't be happening.

"You've worked for Mid-America for decades," I told her. "They can't force you out to make way for her."

"It's what Corporate wants," Inez said.

She got in her car and drove away.

Dorothy Howell

# Chapter 11

I stood there, too stunned to move, and watched Inez drive away. I could hardly take it in. Corporate was forcing her to retire so they could give her job to Sasha?

Every Mid-American branch was allotted a certain number of employees, but we'd had an open slot since our finance rep quit a few weeks ago. There was room for Sasha, both in the office and on the payroll, without Inez leaving. This didn't make sense. All I could figure was that something else was going on. But what?

A wave of panic, anxiety, or something, swept over me, and I felt overwhelmed by everything that had happened in the past few days. Now I had to deal with Inez leaving—which, under other circumstances, I'd be okay with—and working with that horrible Sasha every day.

Normally, at moments like this, I would have gone to my parents' house. Somehow just hanging out there made me feel better. But I couldn't do that tonight, not with this situation with my brother unresolved. Mom would see something was bothering me. She had a way of making me spill my guts, as only a mom can. I'd have told her about Rob being in town and lying about it, and she would have gotten upset. I didn't want that to happen.

Jillian popped into my head. She was my best friend, and even though she was mired in problems of her own, I absolutely had to talk to her. She would listen and help me sort things out.

I felt a little lighter as I headed for my Honda, then stopped in my tracks.

Nick walked toward me.

It took every ounce of mental, physical, and emotional strength I had not to run to him, throw myself into his arms, let him pull me against him and tell me everything was going to be all right. I wanted to do those things. I wanted *him* to do those things, too.

Couldn't we make this work? Wasn't there some way we could put aside our differences?

"We got a break in the case," Nick said when he stopped in

front of me.

He was all business, with not even the faintest hint of a grin. There would be no melting into his arms for me, and he wouldn't likely suggest spending the night with me tonight—both of which were for the best, I told myself.

"A neighbor came forward," Nick said. "He lives two houses down on the other side of the street. He reported that he witnessed someone outside Brett Sinclair's house the night of the murder."

I felt like I'd been slapped.

"What—what time?" I asked.

"Between three and four," Nick said.

I'd been outside Brett's house around that time.

"We got a description," Nick said. "Tall, slender."

I'm tall and slender.

"Dressed in jeans and a dark jacket with the hood up," he said.

That's what I'd had on.

Oh my God, the neighbor had seen *me*.

My head got light.

"This supports the theory that there were two people in the house," Nick said. "This suspect was one of the murderers or, at least, an accomplice."

"Maybe … maybe it was just somebody taking a walk," I managed to say.

"At that hour? Not likely." Nick shook his head. "No murder weapon has been found. This person the neighbor spotted probably walked off with it."

I dug deep, struggling to keep my composure and asked, "Does this witness think he can identify the person?"

"Says he can."

A few stars appeared before my eyes. I swayed and slumped against my car.

Nick grabbed my shoulders. A surge of adrenaline shot through me.

"Are you okay?" he asked.

I shrugged out of his grip and said, "I'm fine. It's just been one of those days."

I felt his gaze on me, but I didn't dare look up. I couldn't take the chance he'd see that I was lying.

"No, it's more than that," Nick insisted. "You're keeping

something from me."

So much for my attempt to hide my feelings.

"What's going on?" he asked, sounding more like a cop than a boyfriend, or even a friend. "Tell me what it is."

I didn't say anything.

He huffed. "Look, Dana, if you're involved—"

"You expect me to answer all your questions, yet you won't do the same for me?" I demanded.

"Not this again," Nick said, shaking his head. "Are things ever going to be easy with you, Dana?"

"They'd be easy if you weren't so secretive and you'd answer my questions when I ask them," I told him.

He stared at me for a few seconds, then said, "I spend my days, all day, every day, solving puzzles, trying to figure out who did what, in which order, and why. I don't want a relationship that's that much work. I want it to be easy."

"*Easy* meaning it's on your terms all the time?" I demanded.

He didn't say anything.

"Well, good luck with that," I told him.

I got into my Honda and pulled out of the parking lot, my emotions raging, see-sawing between outrage and crushing disappointment.

I didn't look in the rearview mirror to catch a glimpse of Nick. I knew things were over between us. It was never going to work. We'd never put our differences aside. I was going to have to get that job in Pasadena—or somewhere—leave, and never look back.

\* \* \*

"How'd it go at work today?" I asked.

"Nobody had heard," Jillian replied. "Thank God my name wasn't mentioned in any of the news coverage."

We were sitting in the living room of her apartment, a sprawling complex not far from mine. I'd called after I left the Mid-America parking lot and asked if I could come by. She'd agreed right away, especially after I'd offered to show up with drive-thru dinner. We'd finished off the chicken and all the fixings, and were now working on Coronas.

I'd come here intending to pour out my problems knowing

she'd make me feel better, as only a best friend can. But I couldn't bring myself to tell her what had just happened between Nick and me. It was too fresh. I felt too raw. And with the aching realization that things were over—really over—between us, all of the other situations in my life paled by comparison and didn't seemed worth mentioning.

"Of course, I had a ton of work to catch up on," Jillian said.

"Nobody asked why you were out for two days?" I asked.

She tipped up her beer and shrugged. "I just said I was sick."

"Have you heard anything new from the detectives?"

"Not a word," she said. "Which suits me fine."

I could see Jillian was feeling better, getting back to her old self. For a few seconds I considered sharing what information I had about the investigation, but was afraid it might send her into an emotional tailspin again.

"I'd better go," I said, finishing my beer.

"Already?"

I hadn't been there long, but I was too keyed up and antsy to sit still. Thoughts were banging around in my head that I didn't want to share with her, and I was afraid something would slip out and upset her if I didn't leave.

I grabbed my handbag and she walked with me to the door.

"Let's go out on Saturday," Jillian suggested. "I feel like my life has been on hold since Sunday night."

"Sure," I said. "We'll find a new place to go. I don't think either of us wants to go to Quota Vino again."

"I'm fine going there. I'm certainly not going to let a jerk like Brett Sinclair keep me away," Jillian said. "I like the place. Everybody is nice. I ran into that guy who works there and he said they missed seeing me."

"What guy?" I asked.

"I don't know his name. The one who busses the tables," she said.

"Flynn? Where did you see him?"

"In the parking lot when I got home tonight," she said. "So we should definitely go back, don't you think? I mean, it was really nice of him to say that. Oh, no, wait, let's make it Friday night and then go shopping on Saturday. Okay?"

At the moment I didn't feel up to partying or shopping but this was the most enthusiasm I'd seen in Jillian for days, so I didn't want to bring her down.

"Sounds good," I said.

I left her apartment and followed the sidewalk through the grounds to the parking lot. It was dark and the security lighting wasn't very good. It reminded me of my own complex and the times I'd pulled into the lot and seen Nick waiting for me.

My feelings lurched between sadness and anger, and I finally settled on anger. It was easier to manage. I decided to take it out on my brother.

I got into my car and called him. He answered right away.

"I know you're in town," I barked.

He didn't respond, but I didn't give him the chance.

"I saw you—twice. You were with some woman," I told him. "What's going on, Rob? What are you up to?"

"It's not what you think," he said.

"Is Denise here with you? Why are you sneaking around? Why haven't you told Mom and Dad you're in town?" I demanded. "And who's that woman?"

"You're just going to have to trust    me."

"Are you kidding me?"

"You haven't told Mom and Dad about this, have you?" he asked.

"After what they went through last fall? Of course not."

"Look, Dana, I'll explain everything," Rob said. "Soon."

"I want to know now," I told him.

"I can't tell you now," Rob said. "Dana, please, just be patient. I'll talk to you soon."

He hung up.

"Oh!"

I banged my fist against the steering wheel and threw my cell phone into my handbag. What was up with men? Why wouldn't they simply answer my questions? How hard was that?

I stewed for a few minutes, then it occurred to me that insisting Rob immediately tell me what I wanted to know was exactly what Nick had resisted. Were they right? Was I too demanding?

This was definitely not something I could face at the moment.

I started the car and drove away.

Where to go, I mused as I waited at the traffic light at the corner. I was too keyed up to go home. My parents' house was off limits. Shopping didn't seem appealing. I wasn't hungry. Of course, if I had a boyfriend, I could go to his place.

My anger spiked again as the image of Nick filled my head. Along with that visual came the tsunami of worry about the Alexa Sinclair murder investigation. A witness had seen someone—me—outside the house and claimed he could make an identification. It was only a matter of time before the detectives figured out who it was, put me in a lineup, and my entire life would be ruined.

I couldn't wait around for that to happen. I had to find Brett.

My best lead at the moment was Pro Auto Repair. Slade had agreed to meet me there tomorrow night. I didn't have that kind of time.

I flipped a U and headed for Devon.

# Chapter 12

Pro Auto Repair was doing a brisk business, considering the late hour. I cruised past their location on White Avenue, then pulled into the parking lot of a warehouse across the street. I shut down the engine and killed the headlights. None of the other businesses were open. Only the security light on the corner was working.

Pro Auto looked as if it had been the corner gas station a couple of decades ago. Now it was surrounded by a tall fence topped with razor wire. The gas pumps were gone, replaced now by about a dozen vehicles awaiting repair. The garage doors were closed but I saw flashes of bright light inside, probably from a welder. Several men were busy moving cars around, others were driving them onto and off of the lot through a wide gate.

With the place this busy and generating a lot of income, coupled with what had to be low overhead, I figured it must be making an exceptional profit. It looked as if Brett had invested in a winner. Maybe he would use some of that money to keep Laurel's kids' café from going under—if anyone ever heard from him again.

I watched the men as they hustled around. It was too dark to see their faces clearly but I felt sure I could spot Brett if he was there. Maybe he was living inside the place. These old gas stations had restrooms and small offices. It was hard to imagine him living under those conditions, but I was sure he'd prefer it to jail.

I settled deeper into the seat, keeping my gaze trained on the garage for any sign of Brett and thinking about what little I'd learned about the case. My mind kept going back to what Nick had told me about the neighbor who claimed to have seen someone outside Brett's house the night of the murder. I'd assumed it was me he'd seen. Now that the shock had worn off, I realized I hadn't really processed the info.

Whoever the witness was apparently hadn't mentioned seeing a car. Mine was parked in front of Brett's house. If I hadn't been so shaken, I would have asked Nick about it.

The witness obviously hadn't thought anything was amiss

when he'd looked out his window and seen someone walk past Brett's house. If so, he'd have called the cops right away. Now I wondered if he could really identify the person, as he'd claimed. After all, it was around three in the morning. He was probably making a bathroom run half asleep and just happened to look outside.

Maybe it wasn't me the neighbor had seen. Maybe it really was the murderer. The description he'd given the police was vague—tall and slender could describe a lot of people, not just me.

Crystal was about my height with the same sort of build. Laurel was slender, and only a couple of inches taller than me. Both of them had motives for murdering Alexa.

Then, too, Gabe and Flynn had criminal records, plus the tall-and-slender description fit them both. Gabe was sort of standoffish, unusually quiet for a bartender. Flynn seemed annoying and kind of weird. But neither of them had a motive—that I'd learned of, anyway—and Gabe's domestic violence arrest fifteen years ago and Flynn's juvenile record were a long way from cold-blooded murder.

It had seemed obvious to me right from the start that Brett, with both the motive and opportunity, had murdered his wife. But I couldn't rule out anyone.

I watched the men at Pro Auto hustle around and thought about how Crystal was still in love with Brett. I wondered if she'd stalked him, driven past his house; it's the kind of thing women did. Had she seen Alexa drive up that night and thought the divorce was off and her chance to get Brett back was gone forever? Had she murdered Alexa to keep that from happening?

Maybe Laurel and Alexa had been in touch; they were, after all, sisters-in-law. Had Laurel learned that Alexa intended to come back home that night? Had she been lying in wait and murdered Alexa so she wouldn't financially ruin Brett—and consequently Laurel—in their divorce?

My cell phone chimed. A text message from Slade popped up that read, "Unlock your doors."

I frowned at the screen. "What the—"

Someone banged on my passenger window. I jumped and saw Slade glaring in at me. I flipped the locks and he dropped into the seat.

"Drive," he told me.

"What's going on—?"

"Drive!"

I started the engine, hit the gas, and swung onto White Avenue.

"Hang a left," Slade told me.

The light turned yellow but I gunned it, heading east on State Street. We drove a few blocks with Slade glancing behind us before he pointed to a Denny's restaurant up ahead and said, "Park in the back."

I swung in, cruised to the rear of the building, and nosed into a spot. Only a few other cars were there, presumably employees. It was dark. Nobody was around.

"What's going on?" I demanded as I killed the engine. ""How did you know I was there?"

He turned sideways in the seat. I thought he wanted to look at me when answering my question but he watched the parking lot instead.

"You're helping your friend and that was your best lead. Where else would you be?" Slade said. "Pro Auto is a chop shop."

"As in cutting up stolen vehicles for parts?" I asked.

"Among other things," he said.

Now I understood why Slade hadn't wanted me coming here at all—and certainly not alone.

"They run cars, trucks, bikes into Mexico. Good money down there for them. Sometimes they bring back drugs and illegals."

This didn't jive with the Brett I knew who frequented a wine bar, lived in an upscale neighborhood, and was a partner in a café that catered to kids.

"Does Brett know he's involved in an illegal operation?" I asked.

"He's cool with it."

Slade had told me Brett was trouble and to steer clear of him. His warning made sense now—and so did everything else.

"That's it," I told him. "That's where Brett is. He took one of the stolen cars and headed for Mexico. That's where he's hiding, which is why the detectives can't find him."

"No," Slade said.

Then something else popped into my head.

"What if Brett screwed over his partners at Pro Auto?" I asked.

"Nobody screws over Pro Auto. Not if they want to keep breathing."

"Brett could have. It's possible," I insisted. "And to get back at him, they murdered his wife."

"No."

"It makes perfect sense," I told him.

"Except for one thing," Slade told me. "Brett's dead."

"He's—he's *dead*?"

"His body was just found," he said. "Best guess is that whoever killed Alexa also killed Brett."

* * *

I offered to take Slade back to wherever he'd left his car but he just climbed out of my Honda and disappeared into the shadows. I grabbed my cell phone and called Nick.

"Why didn't you tell me Brett Sinclair was dead?" I asked as soon as he answered.

"Where are you?"

I huffed. Couldn't he answer a single question I put to him?

"Denny's on State," I told him.

"Stay there." Nick hung up.

Without Slade sitting next to me I didn't feel so great about being parked in this dark, isolated spot, so I drove to the front of the building. Nick was probably home but he might have been working. I had no idea when he'd get here. I went inside, grabbed a booth, and ordered coffee and a slice of chocolate cake. He got there before the food did.

"How did you find out about Brett Sinclair?" Nick asked, sliding onto the seat across from me.

That was it? That was his greeting? No concern for my safety? No thought that I was upset by the news?

I guess it really was over between us.

That would be so much easier to deal with if Nick didn't look so great, of course. He had on jeans and a navy blue polo shirt. I usually saw him dressed in a sport jacket and tie, what I always thought of as detective-wear. But maybe he considered himself on duty right now, despite his casual attire. I had to be careful what I said.

"So it's true?" I asked. "Brett's dead?"

The waitress delivered my cake and coffee.

"Get you something?" she asked Nick.

"Coffee," he said.

When she walked away he said, "A family was looking for their lost dog on the outskirts of Webster."

Webster was east of Santa Flores, a mostly rural area with pockets of tract homes and mom-and-pop businesses. I'd been there many times calling on my customers.

"They spotted the car pulled over to the side of the road, saw a body inside, and called it in," Nick said. "This just happened. I didn't know about it when I saw you earlier."

"And it's really Brett? You're sure?"

"Positive." He nodded. "Preliminary information indicates he'd been dead several days. Probably since the night Alexa was murdered."

The waitress served Nick his coffee and left again.

"This proves Jillian is innocent," I told him.

"How so?" he asked, then grabbed my fork and helped himself to a bite of my cake.

"Come on, you don't really think she murdered Alexa in the kitchen, then killed Brett, loaded him into his car, and drove him all the way out to Webster and left him there, do you?" I asked.

Nick sipped his coffee. "Who do you think killed them?"

I reminded myself not to speak too freely around Nick.

"How would I know?"

"You must have an idea," he said, and forked another wedge of my cake.

Even though Slade had been adamant that Brett would never have crossed his partners at Pro Auto, I figured that a double murder wasn't beyond them.

"It's no secret that some of Brett's business investments were shady," I told him.

"He called nine-one-one," Nick said. "The tape is garbled; reception is bad out there. Only a few words were audible. He was chasing somebody, probably the person who murdered his wife."

"Which proves it wasn't Jillian," I insisted.

"Maybe. Maybe not," Nick said. "Brett must have heard a noise—probably the garage door opening since that's where Alexa's car was found—gone to the kitchen, and walked in on the murder. He gave chase and they ended up out in Webster. There was a confrontation. Brett got the worst of it. All of those things happened before Jillian called to report the crime. It makes her a clear suspect."

"Jillian didn't have her car there, remember?" I reminded him.

"So she claims." He shrugged. "Someone else was in the house, the person whose fingerprints were found. Jillian's accomplice. Brett could have been chasing either one of them."

"But why would Jillian be involved in a murder plot in the first place?" I asked.

"Not my case," Nick reminded me. "I don't have all the evidence."

"I don't need evidence," I said. "I know my friend. She wouldn't murder anyone."

"I agree," Nick said, and scraped the last of my cake off of the plate. "But until the detectives assigned to the case find who's responsible, Jillian will be involved."

I was annoyed with most everyone at the moment—the detectives who apparently refused to see what was so clearly in front of them; the suspects I'd come up with yet had found no evidence against; Brett who was dead and couldn't clear Jillian; my brother who was hiding something from me, and the DM at Mid-America who was forcing Inez to retire.

Most of all I was annoyed with Nick.

I couldn't sit there any longer.

"I've got to go," I said.

I fished a twenty from my handbag, dropped it on the table and left.

"Dana?" Nick called as he followed me out the door.

I stopped and gazed up at him. I'd seen him dozens of times in parking lots. The lighting really worked for him. But seeing how handsome he looked made me sad. In a short while that Pasadena job would likely come through. I'd never see him again—which was the best thing that could happen, I reminded myself.

Nick must have read something in my expression. "Dana—"

"I'm moving," I told him. "I'm up for a job in Pasadena. I should hear from them any day. When I do, I'll leave. Forever."

I caught only a fleeting glance at the stunned look on Nick's face before I whipped around, got in my car, and drove away.

# Chapter 13

I was no more ready to go home now than when I'd left Jillian's apartment earlier and gone to Pro Auto. I cruised down State Street. Luckily, traffic was light, making driving somewhat mindless.

The look on Nick's face was frozen in my mind. What did it mean? Was he upset that I was probably leaving? Shocked? Stunned? Sad?

Or maybe he was okay with it.

I forced him from my thoughts as I turned onto Fleming Avenue. There was nothing I could do about my situation with Nick, but I could use my brainpower to help Jillian. It would certainly be more productive.

According to the homicide detectives' theory about Brett's murder, he'd caught Alexa's killer in the act, given chase, ended up out in Webster where a confrontation had taken place with Brett paying the ultimate price. That scenario made sense.

But would Brett have given chase to anyone on my list of suspects? He knew Crystal, Laurel, Gabe, and Flynn, so why go after them? Why not just call the cops from the kitchen and report who'd murdered Alexa?

Ideas floated through my head as I drove down Fleming Avenue, and the best reason I could come up with was that the murderer had worn a disguise. Not knowing who it was, Brett had followed.

My list of suspects filled my head and once more I considered which of them had the most to gain by Alexa's death. I kept coming back to Crystal. But would she have killed Brett after he'd chased her all the way out to Webster? Possibly, I decided.

Maybe she'd reached her breaking point when he'd caught and confronted her, and realized what she'd done in the heat of the moment. Or perhaps Brett hadn't been happy that Crystal had killed his wife. It was possible he hadn't properly appreciated her attempt to get back into his life, and had threatened to run to the cops rather than into her open arms.

It was all just conjecture on my part, I decided as I stopped at a traffic light. Nick wouldn't likely give me any more info about the case so I had no way of finding out if Crystal had an alibi for the night of the murders.

Unless I asked her myself.

I glanced at the clock on my dashboard. Quota Vino was still open. Figuring I was due for some luck, I continued down Fleming Avenue, then turned onto Sixth Street and found a parking spot in the nearby lot.

When I walked through the door I was glad to see that only a few tables were occupied. Shelly was waiting on one of them. Gabe was behind the bar. No sign of Flynn. Crystal was bussing one of the booths. She glanced up as I approached.

"Grab any table you'd like," she said as she loaded dirty dishes into the plastic bin.

I was tired, annoyed, and not in the mood to finesse a conversation with Crystal. Plus, I didn't know if she'd learned of Brett's death yet. I didn't want to be the one to tell her.

"Where were you the night Alexa Sinclair was murdered?" I asked.

Crystal straightened up and looked at me as if I'd lost my mind.

"You think I killed her?" She shook her head. "Get real."

"Then answer my question," I told her.

"You've got some kind of nerve," she told me, then huffed and said, "I was home. Alone."

"So you don't have an alibi?" I asked.

"I didn't murder Alexa, okay? It wasn't me," she said. "It was over between Brett and me."

Nick flashed in my head. Did you ever really get over somebody you'd once loved?

"I've got work to do," Crystal said.

She grabbed the bin of dirty dishes and walked away.

I was considering going after her when my cell phone chimed. Jillian was calling. I answered as I walked outside.

"Oh my God, have you heard?" Jillian shrieked. "I just saw it online. Brett's dead. He's *dead*."

I didn't want to tell her I'd learned the news earlier. She didn't give me a chance, anyway.

—

"What does this mean?" she demanded, her voice getting higher. "Oh my God, do you think the cops will accuse me of killing him, too?"

Nor did I want to tell her that was exactly what the detectives were thinking.

"They're still gathering evidence," I said as I headed down the sidewalk toward the parking lot where I'd left my car.

"Talk to Nick," she said, sounding more desperate with each passing moment. "Oh my God, you have to talk to him. He can find out what's going on, can't he? I know he can."

"This just happened," I said. "Nobody knows anything yet."

"I'm losing my mind over this thing," Jillian screamed. "I have to talk to you. Where are you? Are you home?"

"No, not yet—"

"Meet me. Please, Dana, I have to see you before I go completely crazy," she said. "Quota Vino. Meet me there. I saw Flynn at Taco Bell a few minutes ago, and he kept going on about how I need to come back, so let's just go there, okay?"

I stopped walking.

"You saw Flynn again?" I asked.

"So, look, I can meet you there in—"

"Didn't you see him outside your apartment, too?" I asked.

"What difference does it make?" she demanded. "Just meet me, okay?"

"How did Flynn know where you lived?" I asked.

"What's the big deal? He lives in the same complex," she told me. "So Quota Vino in twenty minutes. Okay?"

"Yeah, okay."

I ended the call but my thoughts were elsewhere.

When Flynn had stopped me outside my apartment he'd told me he lived there. Now he claimed he lived in Jillian's complex? And he *just happened* to see her at Taco Bell tonight?

The day after Alexa's murder when I'd gone to Quota Vino, Flynn had confronted me outside the restroom after knocking over my drink. He'd seemed angry and had accused me of not being a good friend to Jillian. The exchange had hit a nerve with me; I'd been thinking the same thing. Now I had the creepy feeling that something else had been going on.

I spun around and went back inside Quota Vino.

Crystal stood at the end of the bar waiting for an order. She shook her head when she saw me and said, "What? You suddenly came up with some evidence that proves I killed Alexa and are making a citizen's arrest?"

"What's up with Flynn?" I asked.

She huffed. "Oh, so now you think Flynn killed Alexa, huh?"

"He has a juvenile record," I told her.

"Who doesn't?" Crystal said. "Look, he's a good kid. He lives with his grandma and takes care of her. Would a murderer do that?"

"You seem like you know him pretty well," I said.

"Well enough to know that he comes to work on time, he does a good job, and he doesn't deserve all the things everybody says about him," Crystal said. "Can he help it if people misinterpret his good intentions? He cares about people and watches out for them. Is that so horrible?"

"Some people might call that stalking," I told her.

"Oh, honestly," she grumbled and walked away.

I wound through the tables and out onto the sidewalk. The night air was chilly. Traffic was light. I headed for the parking lot.

Crystal had seemed eager to believe Flynn was a great guy. I couldn't put much stock into her opinion; she'd convinced herself that Brett was a nice guy, too. Something more was going on. I needed to find out what it was.

I called Nick. He answered on the first ring.

"Dana, hi. Listen, I—"

"Flynn's juvenile record. What was in it?"

Nick paused, then said, "What's going on, Dana?"

In a heartbeat he'd switched to his detective voice.

"What was he arrested for?" I asked.

Even though juvenile records were sealed, I was certain Nick had tracked down the detectives who'd handled the case and gotten the details. Nick was that kind of cop. He hadn't given me the information earlier because, really, there was no need, plus I hadn't asked for it. Nick would respect the intent of the sealed records unless there was a great need not to.

I guess he heard that need in the tone of my voice.

"Trespassing," he told me. "Neighbors claimed he was looking in their windows. He'd gotten inside a couple of houses. Nothing stolen or damaged. He just went inside and—"

---

96

I hung up and called Jillian.

Now I was even more creeped out about Flynn. I didn't want Jillian coming out of her apartment tonight to meet me and run into him again. Nor was I crazy about going over to her place thinking I might run into him, but Jillian was so upset I had no choice but to go.

"I'm pulling out of the parking lot now," Jillian said when she answered my call.

Too late, I realized. But at least she was in her car, safe and on the move.

"I don't want to meet at Quota Vino," I told her.

My cell phone chimed. I glanced at the ID screen and saw that Nick was calling. I ignored it.

"Let's go to that place on Fleming," I said. "The new restaurant we tried last week, remember?"

"Okay, if you want," Jillian said. "See you in a few minutes."

We ended the call. My phone chimed, this time with a text message from Nick asking what was going on.

I threw my cell phone into my handbag and hurried to my car.

\* \* \*

"Just when I thought everything might, just might, be okay, now this," Jillian groaned, covering her face with her palms. She looked at me again. "What's going to happen?"

We were seated at a booth in Le Petit Bistro, a new restaurant on Fleming Avenue just a few blocks from Quota Vino. The place had a French flair, with stone walls, dark wood, waiters in berets, and menu items nobody could pronounce. We'd ordered coffee.

"You have to calm down," I told her.

The words came out sounding harsher than I'd meant, but I was a little stressed out, too, after the evening I'd had.

"You're right, you're right." Jillian drew a cleansing breath. "Just tell me what you've learned. Did you talk to Nick?"

I gave her a quick rundown of what he'd told me at Denny's about Brett's murder.

Jillian sighed. "I can't believe he's really dead."

She seemed sad, which surprised me, given what she'd gone

through because of him. Clearly, she was in a more generous mood than I was.

"I need to ask you about Flynn," I told her. "What's going on with him?"

The waiter appeared and served our coffee, then said something in French, I guess, and left.

"With Flynn? What do you mean?" Jillian asked, totally lost. "Nothing's going on. Why would you even ask that?"

I didn't want to alarm her unduly, but I had to tell her what I'd learned.

"I get a weird vibe from him," I said.

Jillian waved away my concern. "He's a nice guy. He slips me free drinks at Quota Vino sometimes. That's all."

"He was outside my apartment the other day. He told me he lived there," I said. "Then he said he lived at your complex."

She sipped her coffee, then said, "Yeah, that's kind of weird."

"It's more than just weird," I insisted.

"Really, Dana, I'm more concerned about the cops showing up at my place and arresting me."

"I think he might be obsessed with you," I said. "He has a juvenile arrest record for trespassing in his neighbors' houses."

"So?"

"So I think maybe Flynn might be involved in Alexa and Brett's murders," I said.

"Because he used to sneak around his neighbors' houses when he was a kid?" She shook her head. "I don't see a connection."

Honestly, after saying it aloud I wasn't sure there was a connection. Jillian was right. It was kid stuff and a long way from murder. Maybe I was looking for something that just wasn't there.

We talked for a while longer, mostly about Jillian being upset and worried, and what might or might not happen. It was nearly midnight when we left.

"You'll let me know if you learn anything new?" she asked, as we crossed the parking lot.

"Sure," I said. "And be careful, okay? Watch out for Flynn. There's something off with that guy."

We got into our cars. I waited until she drove away, then started my car. I couldn't seem to put it in gear.

My suspicion about Flynn wouldn't quit. I needed to find out whether or not he was a stalker, and maybe something worse, but I didn't know how I'd accomplish it. I didn't really want to talk to Nick. Even if I put aside my personal feelings for him, I knew he'd want to know why I was asking and he'd realize I was involved with the investigation. I didn't want to get into it with him, especially after I'd led him to believe I was minding my own business.

Still, I had to do something about Flynn. If the homicide detectives hauled Jillian in for questioning again, I wasn't sure how well she'd hold up.

I pulled my cell phone from my handbag and, ignoring yet another text from Nick, I called Slade.

"I need your help," I said, when he answered. I told him where I was.

"I'm close." He hung up.

Within ten minutes Slade pulled up. He parked and slid into my passenger seat.

"Talk," he said.

I explained about Flynn's arrest record, that I suspected he was obsessed with Jillian and probably stalking her, and added, "I can't shake the feeling that he's involved in Alexa and Brett's murders."

"Like maybe he was at the house and couldn't stand the thought of her being upstairs with Brett?"

"Maybe. I don't know."

Slade shrugged. "He could have broken in, mistaken Alexa for Jillian."

"Then what? Turned on Brett after he chased him down?" I shook my head. "It sounds kind of far-fetched, doesn't it? I mean, the trespassing charges were juvenile stuff. Trespassing doesn't usually lead to murder."

We were quiet for a couple of minutes and I wondered again if I was way off base. Maybe the fact that Flynn was a creepy liar was affecting my judgement.

"Those whack jobs keep trophies. Photos, trinkets. If he's doing what you think, he'll have a stash somewhere," Slade said. "Where does he live?"

"With his grandmother, wherever that is," I said. "I can do a trace on him tomorrow at work. Maybe I can find out."

Slade shook his head. "He's not keeping that kind of stuff

where grandma might stumble over it."

"He has a locker at Quota Vino. We'd need a warrant to open it and there's no way we'll get it," I told him.

The notion of calling Nick again floated through my head. He could get a warrant but he'd need evidence, and there wasn't any. It seemed hopeless.

I sighed. "I don't see how we can get a look inside—"

"Let's roll."

Slade pushed out of my car. I hopped out and followed. We climbed inside his Blazer and he whipped onto Fleming Avenue, turned onto Sixth Street, then drove to the rear of Quota Vino and parked near the employee entrance.

The place was still open so the lot was crowded. Security lighting was almost non-existent. The door was open; sounds and smells drifted out.

Slade didn't say anything when we got out, just walked to the back of the Blazer. He dug through a couple of toolboxes, then grabbed something and headed for the kitchen entrance. As we walked inside I realized he'd grabbed a bolt cutter.

Most of the cooks and kitchen workers didn't bother to look up as we walked past. Steam rose from the pots. Fry pans sizzled. Bits of food littered the floor. I darted ahead of Slade and led the way to the alcove that held the employees' lockers, then pointed to the one with Flynn's name on it.

I was amped up, anxious. I glanced back at the cooks. Two of them were watching us .

Slade fitted the bolt cutters over the lock, snapped it, then tossed it aside and opened the locker. It was empty.

I gasped. "I—I thought sure—"

"Go."

Slade caught my arm and walked me through the kitchen, and outside. We jumped into his Blazer and drove away. I looked back as we turned the corner. One of the cooks was in the doorway watching us.

Neither of us said anything until we got back to the Le Petit Bistro parking lot. Slade killed the engine.

"Wow, was I wrong, or what?" I said. "Sorry I dragged you into this."

"No worries," he said.

I sighed. "I'm going home. It's been a hell of a day."

"Looks like your co-workers are still putting in the hours," Slade said.

He nodded across the parking lot.

I realized the lot adjoined that of the Santa Flores Inn. Sitting directly under a bright security light was Mr. Frazier's bug-green Buick.

"Our district manager is staying here," I said.

"Must be a late night meeting."

He grinned and pointed to the car parked next to Mr. Frazier's.

Sasha's cherry red Lexus.

# Chapter 14

Mid-America had a zero tolerance policy concerning integrity issues. It couldn't afford not to.

In each of its hundreds of branches nationwide, a minimum of two employees had the authority to approve loans and sign company checks. Mid-America was a major corporation; its well of funds was bottomless. Plus, thousands of dollars in customers' payments passed through our hands and into our local bank account each week. The opportunity for an employee to steal from the company on a massive scale was always a threat.

Of course, Mid-America had systems in place to prevent fraud and embezzlement. However, the employees who were qualified enough to have attained loan and check-signing authority were just the kind of people with the inside knowledge necessary to get around these measures.

Coercion was also a problem. If someone unscrupulous uncovered some dirt on an employee in authority at Mid-America, they could blackmail them into embezzling tons of money to keep their secret quiet. It had happened. I'd heard lots of stories about other Mid-America branches, related as cautionary tales of employees who'd been fired, at best, and prosecuted, at worst.

I wasn't hoping for anything that drastic when I walked into the Mid-America office the next morning, but something close to it.

Carmen sat at the front counter opening her cash drawer and Jade was shuffling papers around on her desk. Inez glanced at the clock when I walked past; leave it to her to be diligently adhering to company policy even though she was being forced out of her job. Mr. Burrows' office door stood open and I saw him seated behind his desk with Mr. Frazier standing over him. Sasha was in there, too, pointing at something on the computer screen.

It seemed like the start of typical day—except that, before closing time, somebody was doing down.

Manny was surrounded by stacks of file folders when I reached my desk. I grabbed my cell phone, stowed my handbag, and walked over. When he met my gaze I gave him an urgent eyebrow bob and headed for the breakroom. He got the message and followed.

The breakroom was small but I felt compelled to glance around and make sure it was empty before I leaned close to Manny and whispered, "I know why Mr. Frazier has visited our branch so much lately."

I presented him with my cell phone displaying the photo I'd taken last night of Sasha and Mr. Frazier's cars parked side by side at the Santa Flores Inn.

Manny's eyes bugged out. "Holy crap."

"There's more," I said quietly.

He glanced behind him and moved closer while I paged through the pictures. I'd caught both vehicles, license plates clearly visible, along with the inn's welcome sign and the flashing neon light that displayed the temperature and time—nearly one in the morning.

"And get this," I whispered. "I found out that the DM is forcing Inez to retire so Sasha can have her job."

"That's low, really low," Manny muttered.

"I figure it's just a matter of time before Mr. Burrows is forced out so Sasha can become branch manager," I said.

"Holy crap," Manny whispered. "Frazier will be here all the time. We'll never have a minute's peace."

"I can't let this go," I whispered.

Manny frowned. "You could be opening yourself up for trouble, Dana. A lot of trouble."

"I know."

If I ratted them out, the whole thing could blow up in my face. Whistleblowers weren't always appreciated.

"But what else can I do?" I asked. "How can I know about this, then stand by and do nothing?"

"Tough one." Manny blew out a heavy breath. "Give it some serious thought. Let me know what you decide."

I went back to my desk and, just as I sat down, my cell phone vibrated. Another message from Nick. He'd texted me several times since last night and had left me a couple of voicemails. I hadn't listened to the messages. The texts all said that he needed to talk to me.

If it had been something about Brett's murder investigation—

some new evidence or a major break in the case—Nick would have simply stated it. He probably wanted to know why I'd asked about Flynn's juvenile record, and I wasn't up to dealing with him and whatever he wanted to say about my involvement with the case.

I slid my phone out of sight under a file folder, logged onto my computer, and got to work.

In between phone calls to my customers, thoughts of Flynn swirled around in my head. I'd been so sure he was stalking Jillian and that he was somehow connected to the murders. Was I really wrong about him?

Nick popped into my head. I wondered if he was working on the case, or if he'd gone on with his routine. He'd stopped texting me which, for some reason, was hurtful and at the same time made me angry. I thought about calling him just to yell at him—and that made no sense because, really, I didn't want to talk to him.

The morning ground on. Every time I looked across the office and saw Inez going about her duties, I got mad all over again. Every time I heard Sasha's voice, I wanted to scream at her and tell everybody she was slutting her way up the corporate ladder, starting with Mr. Frazier.

I was counting the minutes until I could leave for lunch when my cell phone vibrated. Mom was calling. I hadn't talked to her in a while and this was just the excuse I needed to slip away for a few minutes. Mom always made me feel better about things. I couldn't tell her what was going on, of course, but I knew hearing her serene voice while she caught me up on her baking and church work would smooth out my day.

I palmed my phone and went to the breakroom.

"Dana, something terrible has happened," Mom wailed, when I answered the phone.

"Oh my God, what is it?" I demanded as I plastered my palm to my forehead and paced across the room. "Is it Dad? Did something happen to him? Is he okay?"

"It's your brother."

I froze and gritted my teeth. I knew something was going on with Rob. Why hadn't he told me what it was when I'd asked? Why had he let me be blindsided like this?

"He's coming home this weekend," Mom told me.

My heart pounded as I waited for the bad news. Mom didn't say anything. I gulped and said, "Yeah? Okay. What's the terrible news?"

"I don't know."

"What?"

I was going to kill my brother when I saw him again.

"Then what makes you think something terrible is happening?" I asked.

"Because he called and talked to your dad," Mom said.

The tension I heard in her voice stressed me out even more. I slumped against the wall beside the refrigerator. Something terrible was definitely happening. Rob never called Dad. He always called Mom. I always called Mom. We both knew that it was pointless to talk to Dad because no matter what was going on, good or bad, he'd tell us to talk to Mom.

"Rob was sick last fall, remember?" Mom said. "He had that flu that just hung on for weeks. I begged him to go to the doctor. I think maybe he's relapsed. What if it wasn't the flu? What if it's Ebola?"

"Mom—"

"Or maybe it's his heart."

"Mom—"

"What if it's cancer—"

"Mom, stop!" I started pacing again. "Stop imagining the worst."

"Oh, Dana, you're right, you're right. It's just that I'm so worried," she said. "Call your brother. Please, call him for me. Find out what's going on. He didn't give your dad any details and, of course, he didn't push for any."

Now she was upset with my dad, which was probably better than her spending the rest of the day composing a mental list of every possible illness on the planet that could have befallen my brother.

"I'll handle it," I told her. "I'll call Rob right now and I'll let you know as soon as I reach him."

"Good. That's good, Dana. Thank you." Mom exhaled heavily. "Let me know right away. Immediately. As soon as you hear something."

"I will," I promised.

I ended the call, then punched in my brother's number. How could he have done this? What was he up to? What was he hiding? And what did he plan to spring on my parents this weekend?

His voicemail picked up.

"Listen to me, you stupid idiot!" I screamed. "Mom is out of her mind with worry! Call me! Now! And I mean *right now!*"

I jabbed the button to end the call, shaking with fury.

"Taking care of personal business on company time?"

I spun around. Sasha stood in the breakroom doorway.

"Handle your family matters on your own time from now on," she told me.

I could have ripped every hair out of her carefully coiffed up-do and thought nothing of it.

Instead, I whipped through my cell phone, found the photos I'd taken last night and put it up to her face.

Her eyes widened.

"Transfer to a different branch," I told her. I was raging inside but managed to sound calm.

She gasped and fell back a step.

"I don't want to see you in here after today," I said. "Got it?"

She just stared.

*"Got it?"*

Sasha met my gaze and gave me the tiniest nod.

I stormed past her, grabbed my handbag, and headed for the door.

"I'm going to lunch," I barked at Inez, and left the office.

* * *

Somehow, I got through the day. I went through the motions of calling my customers and handling problems that arose, but I was so upset by everything that was happening I could hardly think straight. At 5:30, I was the first one out the door. I jumped in my car and headed home.

I wasn't sure if I'd have a job tomorrow. Sasha had likely told the DM about the photos I'd taken of their rendezvous at the hotel. Would he retaliate against me? Fire me? And what would become of my customers if that happened? Who would protect them from Sasha?

The job in Pasadena crept into my thoughts as I merged onto the freeway. What if it fell though? I'd felt good about it, but what if I'd been wrong? Where would I work?

The prospect of being unemployed bore down on me. I'd

have to find another job. What if the only position I could get was in Santa Flores? I wouldn't be able to move and get a fresh start. I'd never be able to stop thinking about Nick. I'd be on that emotional roller coaster forever.

And what if my brother really had cancer? What if Jillian got arrested, then I got arrested? How would my mom manage with a son dying slowly and a daughter behind bars?

My head was starting to hurt. I ran the window down and let the chilly wind blow my hair. When I got home I intended to put on my pajamas, curl up with Seven Eleven, and dive into my emergency carton of chocolate chip ice cream.

By the time I exited the freeway and pulled into my apartment complex, I'd mentally added M&Ms, Oreos, chocolate syrup, and whip cream to what would be tonight's dinner—and realized how badly I'd need it when I swung into a parking space.

Nick stood next to his car.

I wasn't up for this. It crossed my mind to slam into reverse and peel out, and take off for—well, somewhere. Anywhere. Any place where I wouldn't have to keep seeing him and my heart wouldn't keep breaking every time I did.

Didn't he get that? Didn't he understand?

Apparently not, I realized, as I got out of my car and Nick walked over smiling as if he actually thought everything was okay between us.

I kept walking and said, "Has Brett and Alexa's murderer been caught?"

He walked alongside of me. "Why did you ask me about Flynn's juvenile record?"

I stopped and glared up at him. "Can't you ever answer one simple question of mine? Just one?"

"If you know something about him—"

"I don't. Okay?"

I didn't want to be reminded of how I'd been so far out in left field with my suspicion about Flynn. I didn't want to justify my actions to anyone, especially Nick.

I started walking again.

"Listen, Dana," he said, moving along beside me. "That's not what—"

"Has any progress been made in the murder investigation?" I asked. "Any progress at all?"

"No, but—"

"Then we don't have anything to talk about," I said, and climbed the stairs to the second floor.

"Dana, wait."

I didn't wait. I headed down the interior hallway to my apartment with Nick on my heels.

"About this job you mentioned in Pasadena," he said. "I want to—"

"Look, Nick, I've had a really crappy day. I'm tired." I unlocked the door.

"Could I just come in for a—"

"No."

I went inside, slammed the door, and slid the dead bolt into place. Afraid I'd look out the peep hole at Nick, I rushed down the hall to my bedroom.

The light was on.

Flynn sat on my bed.

Dorothy Howell

# Chapter 15

I froze. I couldn't move. My brain locked up. I couldn't seem to process what I was seeing.

"Hi, Dana," Flynn said.

I realized Seven Eleven was on his lap. He stroked her silky fur with one hand; his other was around her neck.

"Nice kitty," he said.

Now I was afraid to move.

"How did—" My voice broke. I drew in a shaky breath and tried again. "How did you get in here?"

"The patio slider," he explained, gliding his palm down Seven Eleven's back.

He must have climbed the patio enclosure of the apartment below mine, reached my balcony, and either forced the door open or broken the glass.

"You were at Quota Vino tonight," Flynn said.

My thoughts raced. Should I make a break for it? Run back down the hall? Could I reach the door, open it, get into the corridor before Flynn caught me? And if I did, what then?

"You broke into my locker." His voice was calm and steady, which made my heart pound harder.

Nick. Where was Nick?

"My friend saw you do it. You were with that big guy," Flynn said.

Was he still here? Outside of my door?

"My friend called and told me what you did," he said.

Or had he given up, gone back to his car and driven away?

"He's a real friend. Not like you."

Flynn drew Seven Eleven closer against his chest, one hand tucked under her, the other still circling her neck.

"You shouldn't have abandoned Jillian like that, left her there to face the police alone."

His words hit me as if I'd been slapped. When I'd seen him at Quota Vino the night he'd knocked over my wine glass, he'd told

111

me what a bad friend I'd been for abandoning Jillian. I'd thought he accused me of that because I'd gone home early and left her there with Brett. Now I realized he'd meant something different.

"You were at Brett's house," I said. "You saw me arrive, go inside."

"And I saw you leave, too." Flynn shook his head. "Bad move on your part. Friends don't walk out on friends. Jillian let you off the hook. She's a real friend, a true friend, because she's a fantastic person."

"How did you know Jillian was at Brett's house?" I asked.

"I saw them leave together. I knew what he had in mind. So I followed them. I wasn't going to leave Jillian, in case she needed me," Flynn said. "Good thing I was there."

I got the sick feeling that I'd been right about Flynn all along.

"You were at the house, watching?" I asked.

Flynn uttered a bitter laugh. "Outside? No. Getting inside some place is no problem."

Revulsion rolled through me at the mental image of Flynn strolling through the house while Jillian was upstairs with Brett.

"Good thing I was there," he said. "That woman—Alexa, his wife—showed up. Who knows what she'd have done when she saw Jillian there. She might have hurt her. She would have hurt her. I know she would have."

"So you stopped her before she could," I said.

"That's what friends do," Flynn told me.

"But then Brett came into the kitchen," I said.

"I'd left my car around the corner. I got to it pretty quick and drove off. Then I saw him following me." Flynn shook his head. "He must have really cared about his wife to go to all that trouble—but what about Jillian? He claimed he was crazy about her. I heard him at the wine bar flirting with her, complimenting her, saying nice things to her."

"He followed you out to Webster," I said.

"I *led* him to Webster," Flynn told me. "I go out there a lot. Not many people live there. Small clusters of homes. People feel safe. They don't always close their blinds or lock their doors."

"So you pulled over? You got out of the car. You confronted Brett," I said. "And then you ..."

Flynn rose from the bed. He seemed taller, stronger, here in the close confines of my bedroom.

"This is all your fault, Dana," Flynn told me. "If you hadn't left Jillian at the wine bar, none of this would have happened."

He'd murdered two people. I wasn't waiting around. I knew I was next.

I bolted out of the room and ran down the hallway. Seven Eleven shrieked. Halfway to the kitchen, Flynn grabbed me from behind and shoved me against the wall. I hit hard, bounced, and fell to the floor. He leaned down to grab me again. I kicked his belly, a glancing blow. He dropped to one knee. I screamed and scrambled to my feet. His hand locked around my ankle. I screamed and fell again.

I rolled onto my back, kicking at him furiously. He let go. I crawled away and struggled to my feet. I made it to the door. My fingers grazed the dead bolt slide. Flynn looped his arm around my waist and dragged me through the living room. The patio slider stood open. The drapes billowed in the breeze.

He was going to throw me off the balcony.

I dug my nails into his arm, kicked, twisted, jabbed my elbows into him, and screamed. I wasn't going down without a fight, and I was going to make sure anyone within earshot knew this was no accident.

I heard pounding, shouts, then wood splintering. My front door shattered. Nick burst into the living room.

He went for his gun but Flynn hoisted me higher as he edged backwards toward the slider. I reached back and raked my fingernails across his face.

Flynn pushed me down. I hit the floor hard. Nick rushed forward and grabbed him. They struggled. Flynn threw a punch. Nick ducked. Flynn darted onto the patio. He grasped the railing and climbed over. His hand slipped. Nick grabbed for him but couldn't reach him. He fell.

I rushed onto the balcony. Nick leaned over the railing.

"Is he—is he—?"

Nick gathered me into his arms and turned me away.

"He hit the sidewalk," he said, as he pulled his cell phone from the pocket of his sport coat.

I looked up at him. "So he ... he's ..."

Nick thumbed his cell phone as he hustled me into my living room. Seven Eleven peeked around the corner and trotted toward me. I burst into tears.

\* \* \*

"Make it quick, okay?" Jillian said and gave me a little smile. "You know how you are."

I managed a half-smile in return and said, "Don't worry. I'll be in and out in less than five minutes. I have to do this in person."

We were sitting in Jillian's Toyota in the Mid-America parking lot the next morning. I'd called her last night when the detectives, the techs from the lab, and the people from the coroner's office had showed up at my apartment. She'd come over right away, no questions asked. That's what friends do.

I'd been a complete mess so she'd grabbed a few of my things—along with Seven Eleven—and taken us to her place. I didn't know how I'd ever be able to live in my apartment again after what happened.

When I got out of the car I saw that neither Sasha's red Lexus or the DM's green Buick were in the parking lot. Maybe they were sleeping in. Or maybe they were conspiring with the corporate office to fire me.

Carmen gave me a bright smile when I walked inside. Jade was sipping coffee and fiddling with her cell phone. Mr. Burrows' door was closed. Inez gave me stink-eye as she glanced at the wall clock, then made a note on her calendar that I was six minutes late.

Manny looked up from his desk as I approached. He did a double-take and frowned.

"What's wrong?" he asked.

"Rough night," I said, and gave him a rundown of what happened. "I need to take a couple of days off."

"Sure, Dana, whatever you need," Manny said. "Are you okay?"

I'd sustained a few bruises and bumps last night, but nothing that required medical attention. What I needed most was time to process everything that had happened, and to figure out what to do next.

"Where are Sasha and the DM?" I asked.

Manny smiled. "First thing this morning, Mr. Burrows announced that Sasha is going to work in the Riverside branch and Inez isn't retiring."

"Dana?" Carmen called. "You have a phone call."

"I'm guessing you had something to do with that," Manny said.

I couldn't help smiling. It looked as if my customers would be spared the wrath of Sasha when the Pasadena job came though.

"Dana?" Carmen called again.

"Go. Take care of yourself. I'll handle the call," Manny said. "Carmen, which line?"

"Line two," Carmen said. "It's her brother."

Anxiety shot through me. Leaving Jillian's apartment, I'd seen on my cell phone call log that Rob had tried to reach me. I'd wanted to wait until I got things settled with Manny before tearing into Rob for worrying Mom so much. But now he was calling me at work—and he never called me here—which made me think maybe something terrible really was going on with him.

I hurried to my desk, grabbed the phone, and I steeled myself for the worst.

"Hey, sis, thanks for the loving message you left me yesterday," he said and chuckled.

He didn't sound like he was dying of anything, so I relaxed a little.

"I wanted to surprise everybody," Rob said. "But since Mom is so worried, I'll tell you what's going on. Keep it to yourself, though, okay? Just assure her everything is fine. I want to see her face when I give her the news."

"What news?" I asked.

"Denise and I are moving back to Santa Flores," Rob told me. "You're going to be an aunt."

"I am? *I am?*" I hopped up and down. "Are you serious? Really?"

"Yep," Rob said. "The woman you saw me with was the Realtor. Denise isn't feeling great—you know, morning sickness—so I've been here house hunting this week. She's coming down tonight and we're giving Mom and Dad the news."

"You could have told me what was going on," I said.

"Like I said, we wanted to surprise everybody."

"Well, I'm surprised. I'll tell Mom everything is okay with you but I won't let on what's happening."

"Good. See you tonight," he said.

I hung up the phone and shouted, "I'm going to be an aunt!"

Everybody turned my way. Carmen beamed. Inez glanced at

the clock.

"Congratulations," Manny said and walked over. He nodded toward the door. "Go on. Get out of here. Get some rest and celebrate with your family."

"My parents are going to be thrilled," I said.

Something resembling a blonde tornado caught my eye. Jade rose from her desk chair, preening and tossing her hair from side to side. I expected to see Slade walking through the front door.

It was Nick.

I didn't know if I was up to talking to him.

It seemed I didn't have a choice.

He strode across the front of the office, past the front counter, and directly to my desk. He stopped, his jaw set, his brows pulled together.

Jillian was behind him and said, "I called him. You two need to talk."

"We need to talk," Nick barked.

When I'd left my apartment with Jillian last night, Nick and I hadn't had time to discuss what had happened. I guess we both needed to clarify some details.

"Last night, you came back. How did you know something was wrong?" I asked.

"Listen, about this move you think you're making," Nick said.

"Move? What move?" Manny asked.

"Could you just answer my question?" I said.

"I heard you scream," Nick said.

Carmen hurried to my desk. "You're moving?"

"I don't want you taking that Pasadena job," Nick told me.

"Another job?" Manny asked. "In Pasadena?"

Jade wiggled in between Manny and Nick, and ran both hands through her hair. "Does Slade know?"

"I couldn't leave last night," Nick said.

"Dana?" Inez called, looking at me over her half-glasses. "Are you taking this time off of your lunch hour?"

"Not until we talked," Nick said.

"Maybe I'll give Slade a call," Jade said, and grabbed the phone on my desk.

"Talk about what?" I asked.

"I can't believe you're really thinking about leaving," Manny grumbled.

Nick drew in a breath and straightened his shoulders.

"Do you know why I dated Katie Jo Miller back in high school and not you?" he asked.

"Not this again," I said.

This was hardly the topic I expected to discuss, or even wanted to. The rumor that Nick had gotten my best friend pregnant, made her have an abortion, then dumped her and left town had been the root of all our problems, and was hardly relevant any longer.

"Hear him out, Dana," Jillian said. "Really, you should."

"Do you know why I dated Katie Jo and not you?" Nick asked again.

"We put that to rest," I told him.

"I'll tell you why. Because I knew you'd be a lot of work," he said. "And you are."

"*What?*" I demanded. "I've been trying to get you to discuss our relationship and *that's* what you want to tell me?"

"It's true. You are," Nick said.

"Yeah, you kind of are," Jillian said. "At times."

"I don't want to have to hire somebody new," Manny moaned.

"I don't believe this," I said.

"I'll check with Corporate and see if we're allowed to hire a new employee," Inez said.

Nick held up both hands, as if that would calm me down.

"I came to see you last night because I realized how much I didn't want you to leave," Nick said. "No relationship is perfect. Ours certainly isn't."

"Oh, thanks," I said.

"I didn't know you were dating someone, Dana," Carmen said. "Why didn't you tell me?"

"I realized that relationships are always work," Nick said.

"Well, hello, Slade," Jade cooed into the phone as she fluffed her hair. "It's Jade. Listen, I thought it would be—hello? Hello?"

"I realized something else," Nick said. "You're worth it."

"What ... what are you saying?" I asked.

"Where is my new-hire checklist?" Inez mumbled.

"I think we can learn to compromise," Nick said. "I could be more forthcoming if you didn't insist on knowing absolutely everything."

"That sounds like you want to tell me things when it suits you," I said. "I'm not signing up for partial disclosure."

"You're not exactly forthcoming all the time, either," he pointed out. "You were more involved in the Alexa Sinclair murder investigation than you admitted."

He had me on that and, really, he was right.

"What I'm asking is that you have some faith that I know what I'm doing and it's the right thing," Nick said. "I'm asking that you trust my judgement."

"You'd have to trust my judgement, too," I told him.

He paused, then nodded. "I can do that. Can you?"

"Oh my God, I don't believe this," Jade said, punching the phone again. "Our call must have gotten dropped."

"Maybe I could learn to trust your judgement," I said. "But why should I?"

The door to Mr. Burrows' office opened. He stepped out, took one look around the office, then went back inside and closed the door.

"Because I came to your apartment last night to tell you—"

Nick stopped and looked around. Everybody was staring.

He held out his hand and said, "Let's go outside."

"What for?" I asked. "I don't understand—"

"Dana, this would be one of those times when you should trust my judgement," he said. "Okay?"

I hesitated a moment, then placed my hand in his and said, "Okay."

"Why isn't he picking up?" Jade complained.

Inez glanced at the wall clock as Nick and I walked past her desk. Carmen and Jillian went into a huddle and started whispering. Manny dropped into his chair and mopped his brow.

When we got outside Nick stopped at the corner of the building, faced me and took both of my hands. He looked at me for a few seconds, then drew a deep breath.

"The reason I went to your apartment last night was to tell you I'm in love with you."

"You're—you're what?"

"You can't move to Pasadena, Dana. When you told me about the job there, I … well, I knew it would be the biggest mistake of my life if I let you go."

I was too stunned to say anything.

"We can work this out. We can compromise. Jillian mentioned you're taking off a few days. I'll take some time off, too. I know you don't want to go back to your apartment. You can stay at my place." Nick grinned and rushed to add, "So I can answer all those questions I know you have for me."

I couldn't help grinning, too.

"I love you," Nick said. "Give us a chance."

How could I take the job in Pasadena and move after everything that had happened? I was going to be an aunt. Everything was back to normal at Mid-America. My best friend lived here.

Nick lived here.

He'd promised to compromise, and all he'd asked in return was that I do the same. He seemed so sure we could do it. He'd said all the right things, including that he loved me—something I'd been waiting to hear since high school.

"Will you stay, Dana?" he asked.

I threw my arms around his neck.

"Yes!"

It was an easy choice.


The End

Dear Reader:

I hope you enjoyed Fatal Choice!

If you'd like to know how it all began for Dana and Nick, you can find out in Fatal Debt. Their story continues in Fatal Luck.

You'll probably also like my Haley Randolph mystery series. Haley is an amateur sleuth whose passion for designer handbags leads to murder.

If you're a romance reader, I also write historical fiction under the pen name Judith Stacy.

More information is available at www.DorothyHowellNovels.com and www.JudithStacy.com, and at my DorothyHowellNovels fan page on Facebook. You can follow me on Twitter @DHowell Novels.

Happy reading!
Dorothy

**Ready for more mystery in your life?**

The Haley Randolph mysteries are laugh-out-loud funny and feature an amateur sleuth whose passion for designer handbags always leads to murder!

Praise for the Haley Randolph series:
"A treat for those with a passion for fashion. No doubt this sassy heroine's in for a long run."
—Kirkus Reviews

"A quick read with lots of humor."—Booklist

"A solid mystery"—Publishers Weekly

"Haley Randolph is a hoot. There is no way to get through Howell's latest without laughing out loud at least once a chapter."—Romantic Times

## FANNY PACKS AND FOUL PLAY
### A Haley Randolph Mystery

### Chapter 1

"I'd die for a new handbag," Marcie said.

I was ready to kill for one but didn't say so. Marcie had been my best friend since forever. She already knew.

We were at the Galleria in Sherman Oaks, one of L.A.s many upscale areas, scoping out the shops and boutiques. Marcie and I shared a love—okay, it was really an obsession, but so what—of designer handbags      .

All things fashion-forward were of supreme interest to us. But that was to be expected. We were both in our mid-twenties, smack in the middle of our we-have-to-look-great-now-before-it's-too-late years. Marcie was a petite blonde, and I, Haley Randolph, was tall with dark hair. Marcie was sensible and level headed, and I—well, I wasn't. But that's not the point. We're still BFFs and that's what matters.

Since we'd exhausted all the places we should have been able to find a terrific handbag, we moved through the open-air shopping center past the stores, restaurants, and office spaces toward the parking garage. I had on a fabulous black business suit, since I was on my lunch hour, and Marcie had taken the day off from her job at a bank downtown so she had on jeans, a sweater, and a blazer. We looked great—perfect for a November afternoon.

"What the heck is wrong with all the designers?" I asked, as we passed one of the boutiques we'd already checked out. "All they have to do is design handbags. That's it. And I haven't seen one decent bag in months."

"It hasn't been months," Marcie pointed out. "Only a few weeks."

She was right, of course. Marcie was almost always right.

I was in no mood.

"You've been kind of crabby lately," Marcie said, as only a BFF can. "What's wrong?"

"Nothing," I insisted.

Marcie gave me a we're-best-friends look which was usually comforting, but not today. My life had been a roller coaster for a while now, but I'd been doing okay with it. I had a great job as an event planner at L.A. Affairs and ... and ...and—wait. Hang on. Was that the only good thing I had going?

Oh my God. It was.

I still had my will-this-nightmare-ever-end part-time sales clerk job at the how-the-heck-does-this-crappy-place-stay-in-business Holt's Department Store. My mom was driving me crazy—no, really, crazier than usual—over prep for her upcoming Thanksgiving dinner that I was expected to attend. I'd broken up with my hot, handsome, fabulous official boyfriend Ty Cameron. I was staring down the barrel of the single girl's Bermuda Triangle of holidays—Christmas, New Years, and Valentine's Day—and lately it seemed that if civilization were dying, men would rather let it go than date me.

So was it too much to ask that a designer somewhere come up with a fabulous new handbag that would soothe my worries, boost my spirits, and keep me going until things turned around?

Apparently, it was.

"If you want to talk, I'll be home late tonight," Marcie said. "I'm having dinner with Beau."

Oh, yeah, and Marcie had a new boyfriend—which I'm really happy about. Really.

"Have fun," I said, which I totally meant.

Marcie had kissed her share of frogs, and while Beau might not be her prince, he was at least a really nice guy, good looking with a great job, and liked to go places and do things with her—which was why I was really happy for her. Really.

We waved good-bye and Marcie continued on toward the parking garage. I headed the other way through the Galleria and crossed the busy Sepulveda and Ventura intersection to the building that housed L.A. Affairs, an event planning company to the stars—and everyone else who mattered in Hollywood and Los Angeles. It was my job to execute fabulous parties for people who had more money than they knew what to do with so they spent it on extravagant, outrageous, mine-is-better-than-yours events, then left it up to me to, somehow, pull it off.

I took the elevator up to the L.A. Affairs office on the third floor and walked inside. A florist on our approved list—who wanted us to keep booking them for events—had decorated the lobby with pumpkins, corn stalks, and mum plants.

Mindy, our receptionist, was at her post. She was somewhere in her forties, with a waistline that attested to her total commitment to the Food Network, and blonde hair she's sprayed into the shape of a mushroom.

If it's true that we learn from our mistakes, Mindy will soon be a genius.

"Are you ready to party?" Mindy exclaimed.

She's supposed to chant that ridiculous slogan to clients, yet for some unknown reason I was continually bombarded with it.

"I work here," I told her, for about the zillionth time. "Okay? I'm an employee. Here. You don't have to keep saying that to me."

Mindy made a pouty face and shook her head. "Oh, dear, someone is having a bad day."

I walked away.

Just past the cube farm and the client interview rooms I turned down the hallway where the offices, supply room, conference rooms, and breakroom were located. I desperately needed to hit the snack cabinet. I was long overdue for a chocolate fix, and the mocha frappuccino—the most fabulous drink in the world—that I'd gotten after lunch at Starbucks—the most fabulous place in the world—had worn off.

I ducked into my private office—a great space with neutral furniture and splashes of blue and yellow, and a huge window with a view of the Galleria—and was about to drop my handbag into my desk drawer when my cell phone rang. It was Mom.

Oh crap.

"Good news," she announced when I answered.

Mom's news was seldom good—for me, anyway.

"I've figured out how to remedy my seating chart problem," she said

Mom said it as if she'd just hammered out a peace treaty in the Middle East, and while she did wish for world peace—she was, after all, a former beauty queen—I'm not sure she was even aware there were problems in that region of the world.

Really, how could she know if it wasn't covered in *Vogue*?

"Oh?" I murmured, as I dropped into my desk chair.

"I've been quite concerned about your sister lately," Mom said.

To the untrained observer, it appeared that Mom's seating chart and her concerns for my sister weren't related. I knew the connection would be revealed—as long as I was patient enough to wait.

I'm not usually that patient.

"She hasn't been herself since she broke up with Lars," Mom said.

I had no idea who Lars was.

My sister was a little younger than me. She attended UCLA, did some modeling, and was a near perfect genetic copy of our mother.

I wasn't.

"So," Mom said, "I'm going to find a dinner companion for your sister on Thanksgiving."

I lurched forward in my chair. She was going to—what?

"That way she won't be lonely and sad," Mom said.

She was going to set up my sister with a blind date?

"Someone from a good family, of course," Mom said. "Young and handsome, well educated."

What about me? She knew I'd broken up with Ty.

"Which will also solve my seating chart problem," Mom said.

No way did I want my mother to set me up with somebody— but that's not the point.

"I'm calling around now to see who's eligible," Mom said. "I'll let you know."

She hung up. I jabbed the red button on my cell phone and tossed it into my handbag.

Oh my God, I couldn't believe this. My life was locked in a death spiral and *this* was what Mom wanted to do?

The office phone on my desk rang. It was Mindy.

"Hello? Hello? Haley?" she asked, when I picked up.

I drew a quick breath, trying to calm myself.

"Yes, Mindy?"

"Oh, yes, hello. I'd like to speak to Haley," Mindy said.

Good grief.

"I'm Haley," I said.

"Oh, jiminy, so you are," Mindy said and giggled. "So, anyway, there's a Mr. Douglas in the office—no, he's on the phone. Yes, he's on the phone, holding. He wants to come by and see you right now."

A man wanted an appointment? In person? Immediately?

That could only mean one thing—he wanted to plan a surprise party for his wife or girlfriend. Somebody he desperately loved, thought the world of, wanted to impress and flatter, and shower with special moments.

No way.

"Tell him to forget it," I barked, and hung up.

Two people had told me today that I was in a crappy mood. Well, screw them.

I grabbed my handbag and an event portfolio and left.

* * *

Dorothy's books are available in hardcover, paperback, and ebook editions online, at your favorite bookstore, and on all ebook platforms.

Get the latest news at www.DorothyHowellNovels.com, and www.JudithStacy.com, on her Dorothy Howell Novels Facebook page, and follow her on Twitter @DHowellNovels.

Dorothy Howell writes for two major publishers, in two genres, under two names. She's published 39 novels. Dorothy pens the hilarious Haley Randolph mysteries, as well as the Dana Mackenzie series. She writes historical romance under the name Judith Stacy. Dorothy lives with her family in Southern California.

CPSIA information can be obtained
at www.ICGtesting.com
Printed in the USA
LVHW080116021020
667693LV00011B/1127